SPEED SKATING

CHICAGO VELOCITY
BOOK 2

ABBY BURCH

Copyright © 2023 Abby Burch
All rights reserved.
Trademarks used herein are owned by their respective trademark owners and are used without permission.
No part of this publication may be reproduced in whole or in part, or stored in a retrieval system, or transmitted in any form or by any means, electronic, mechanical, photocopying, recording, or otherwise, without written permission of the author.
This is a work of fiction. Any and all likenesses to real people or events are purely coincidental.

Alpha edits by Melissa McGovern, @chapters.and.charcuterie
Proofreading and editing by Cait Marie, caitmarieh.com
ARC management by Jamie Davis, @babewithbigbooks

ISBN: 9798738847967

PREFACE

This book contains mentions of the past death of a parent. It also has on-page discussions of mental health, including depression and grief.

SPEED SKATING PLAYLIST

I'm excited to share a few of the songs I had on repeat while writing this book. Some of these breathed life into the manuscript early on (Mae's "Multisensory Aesthetic Experience" album in particular) and others came into play much later on. Regardless, they all got a lot of love from me as Morgan and Nils came to life on the page.

- Our Love is a Painted Picture | Mae
- Seconds Away | Thomston
- See Her On The Weekend | Andrew McMahon in the Wilderness
- Bloom | Mae
- The Tension And The Terror | Straylight Run
- Holes in the Sky | M83

- Time in a Bottle | Jim Croce
- Firearm | Lizzy McAlpine
- We Looked Like Giants | Death Cab for Cutie
- Butterfly | Ian Love

For me,
because I earned it.

1

NILS

I have three favorite things.
Number one: Playing hockey.
Number two: Going fast.
Number three: Making love to beautiful women.

The first two have more in common than you'd initially think. The deep roar filling my ears. The wind pressing against my face. And, best of all, the rush of adrenaline pounding through my veins. It never gets old to fly down the ice and slap the puck past the opposing team's goalie into their net. The same as it never gets old hopping on my black Ducati 1299 Superleggera and hitting the freeway, the wind whipping through my hair and the throaty engine opening up under me, filling my entire body with its energy.

My bike, like my skates, gives me freedom from the responsibility and trials in life. When I'm racing down the ice or racing through traffic, there is nothing but the wind and the sound of my heartbeat pounding in my ears. Any reprieve from the voice in my head is a welcomed break, so I drive hard and skate even harder.

As for the third… there certainly isn't a shortage of beautiful women in my life. Being a professional hockey player for the Chicago Velocity means there are always gorgeous ladies around who are looking for a good time. The puck bunnies are young and thin, with big fake tits, perfect fake tans, and zero personality. They're shallow and petty and a dime a dozen. I've fucked a fair number of them, sure, because who hasn't? However, no matter how beautiful they are or how desperate they are for a taste of me, it always still feels like something is missing.

I RACE DOWN I-290, weaving in and out of the inner two lanes of traffic. It's late, and it's fucking cold, but I don't care. Any chance to ride is one I welcome. Thankfully, it hasn't snowed in several days, so the road is dry, allowing me to take the bike for a spin, even though it's February.

She roars beneath me, teasing me with unleashed power and potential. I know that I'm only going about a hundred and forty kilometers per hour, nowhere near the top speed for this beauty, but as much as I love going fast, I would also love not to be a splatter of blood and bone fragments on the pavement tonight. So, I keep it reasonable, obeying speed and traffic laws, and enjoy the opportunity to ride.

The downtown skyline comes into view, and even after three years with the Velocity organization, I'm still in awe of Chicago. Sure, my home country of Sweden has plenty of beautiful, old Nordic architecture, but Chicago is so unique and intriguing to me. It's as if when the city was taking shape, the builders were all competing with each other over who could build the biggest, most interesting building. So many of the structures back home predate the ones in Chicago by multiple generations, and the differences in materials, style, and execution always fascinates me. At night, though, this city truly shines – literally. It never sleeps.

I let off the throttle a bit and stare at the glittering lights in the distance. The city's tallest building, the Willis Tower, looms as I approach, lit from top to bottom at all hours. The top of it pops in and out of the low clouds rolling over the city.

I slow as the freeway ends in downtown, eventually turning north onto Lake Shore Drive. I follow the winding road along the coast of Lake Michigan, its partially-frozen waters inky-black in the night.

When I finally pull into the garage behind my house in the Lincoln Park neighborhood, I can no longer feel any of my extremities. I glide the bike into my dedicated parking spot and kill the motor, the last of its throaty growl echoing through the concrete structure. I pull the helmet off, shaking my head to free my blond hair from its sweaty, flattened mess, and head inside.

Finding a place in Chicago close to the arena and with a private garage was not easy, but I refused to keep my bike in a storage unit or garage far away from me, and this newly remodeled row house fit the bill. I felt comfortable purchasing this place after finally becoming a real member of the team at the end of last year and not constantly being shipped between the Velocity and our farm team in the suburbs.

I'm only twenty-four, so I'll become a restricted free agent in a couple years, but I really love playing here in Chicago. The city, the team, the fans – this is my home because they are all part of me.

2

MORGAN

Bzzt bzzt.

"Ugh, Patrick!" I groan as I roll over, the blankets twisting around my legs, and feel around for my phone on the nightstand. He knows I wanted to sleep in today, so I'm sure it's him who texted me, just to be a jerk.

Despite it being a cloudy morning, the light filling my room is still too bright, and I have to blink a few times while my eyes adjust. I sit up in bed and grab my phone. I open the message to find a photo of a flyer for a fundraiser his hockey team, the Chicago Velocity, is doing for a local children's hospital this weekend. The accompanying message says:

> Be there or be square, loser.

So loving of him.

As the sister of the team captain, who also lives with him, I am highly involved in the world of professional hockey. Since Patrick doesn't have a girlfriend and Mom still lives back home in Minneapolis, I get to be his fill-in plus one for team events. Not that I'm complaining. My brother is my favorite person, although we annoy each other to no end. He's my protector, even when I don't need it. He's my confidant, even when he doesn't want to hear it. And he's definitely someone I'm lucky to have in my life.

Every year, the team does a bowling fundraiser. It's one of the smaller, more low-key events, but it's still a good cause. I had fun at last year's event, and it's such great PR for the team too. It's a win-win for everybody involved.

I put the event into my phone's calendar app before texting Patrick back:

> I'll be there, and I'm gonna kick your ass this year.

Then, I toss my phone back onto the nightstand, roll over, and doze off.

A FEW DAYS LATER, I show up to the event with Patrick on a blustery winter day. I'm in my favorite pair of skinny jeans and one of my many Velocity sweatshirts under my winter travel coat. Once we're inside, I quickly shed the coat and try to smooth out my hair from the mix of wind and static. My long bangs are clipped back to keep them out of my face while I bowl. I got bored and chopped my dark hair into a bob last year, and although I love it, sometimes it's a pain when I want to do various activities. I reaffix my clips as I follow Patrick to the large folding table that is set up next to the shoe rental counter.

One of the marketing team members checks us in on an iPad while another snaps photos.

"Patrick, we have you on lane three with the Cargills," the guy with the iPad says over the sound of bowling balls hitting pins and a group cheering loudly.

Patrick nods his head. I don't know how he is always as cool as a cucumber because I'd be nervous as hell to have to spend the next two hours with the team's owners, but that's why he's the captain.

The marketing guy hands me my VIP badge and some info on the organization we're raising money for. "Morgan, I know you probably want to be with your brother, but we had an uneven number of participants this year, so we assigned you to lane twenty-nine with Larsson. Is that all right?"

I don't know Nils Larsson very well, but I'd definitely *not* like to be on lane three with the owners. Too much pressure for me. "That's completely fine," I assure him.

Patrick and I pose for a quick photo together before he turns to me. "Anybody gives you any trouble or tries to be weird with you, you tell me, okay?"

I roll my eyes. "Patrick, I'm twenty-two years old, and everyone here knows me. I'm sure I'll be fine. You don't have to be so overprotective; I can take care of myself."

"You know I have to look out for you, Morgs. I love my teammates, and we're all like family, but some of these guys are real dogs when it comes to women. You don't hear the way they talk about you."

I'm well aware of the lewd things that have been said about me by some of the guys. Some of them have been ballsy enough to openly hit on me; others have tried to slide into my DMs. The minute Patrick gets wind of any of it, he shuts it down. Most of them back off pretty quickly when he confronts them about it, but he did have to punch one guy in the face who wouldn't leave me alone.

"I'm a big girl. I'll be fine for two seconds without you."

He gives me a hug. "Sorry. You know I can't help but be protective of my little sis."

"I know," I say, squeezing him back. "See you later."

We separate, and he heads down to the opposite end of the alley, where the Cargills are surrounded by other bigwigs in the organization. I'm so glad I don't have to be one hundred percent poised and perfect today since I'm on the other end of the alley. It can be exhausting living up to the expectations set for me as the captain's sister, but I'll happily do what's needed to help him succeed.

A few minutes later, with bowling shoes in hand, I am picking out a bowling ball to use. I settle on a neon pink one and grab it from the rack.

"I didn't take you for the type of girl who likes pink," says a quiet but heavily accented voice from behind me. I spin around to face Nils Larsson.

"That's because I'm not," I tell him matter-of-factly. "However, I'm highly superstitious, and I bowl better with pink balls." He simply nods, accepting my answer, and steps around me to get one of his own.

One of the guys, Matus, on the lane next to us yells, "We all know that's a lie! You prefer blue balls!"

Because he and I are cool with each other, I give him the middle finger in return.

I pop the offensively pink ball onto the return and program our names into the computer. It takes entirely too long to do because this alley hasn't been updated since before I was born. The letters on the buttons are all halfway rubbed off, and I have to hit them with real force to get it to register. Nils's name ends up being NIILS, and I can't make it get rid of the extra I. While I'm wrestling with the machine, he places his black bowling ball into the return and chats casually with Matus and his lane partner, who I'm pretty sure is a random puck bunny because I've never seen her before.

"Ready to roll," I tell Nils.

He glances at his misspelled name on the ancient TV monitor suspended above the lane and scrunches his nose at it, a half-smirk of amusement crossing his face. "Are you sure those fat fingers are going to fit in the holes of your bowling ball?" he quips, taking a seat at the table behind me.

I roll my eyes at him. "Asshole. Take it up with the bowling alley owners. Their equipment is ancient."

He chuckles in response as he pulls a hair tie from his wrist to put up his shoulder-length blond hair.

I turn around and line up for my shot, putting my foot on the painted mark on the floor and making sure my grip is good. I take a breath to steady myself and step forward, swinging the ball back and then forward as I hit the mark just before the foul line. But as I go to release it, the clicking of cameras pulls me out of my concentration, and the ball almost immediately ends up in the gutter. Sighing, I watch as it bounces down the gutter and to the side of the pins hitting none of them.

I know it's a charity event, so there has to be plenty of photos and videos to promote the event, but seriously? I let out another sigh and walk back to the return. I can feel a few sets of eyes on my back as I line up for my next attempt. Unfortunately, my next shot isn't much better, only knocking down two pins.

"Okay, I need a drink," I tell Nils as he's lining up for his first shot. His hair is pulled back into a loose bun. "You want anything?"

"No, thank you," he replies. I head up to the bar and get myself a beer, saying hi to a couple of the hockey wives on the way. Most of them don't participate in the charity events, but rather they come and watch. They're probably afraid of breaking a nail or getting foot fungus from the bowling shoes or something petty like that.

Not that I dislike them. For the most part, they're okay. They just aren't really my type of people.

After getting my drink, I get stopped by one of the team's social media people for a photo op. I quickly throw on a smile next to one of the other hockey wives. The photographer, a tall, blond girl named Sydney Downing, snaps a photo and thanks us.

When I finally get back to the lane, Nils is sitting

again, talking with the girl Matus brought. The screen shows that he bowled a strike. "Damn," I say, setting my beer down. "Apparently, you came to play."

He smirks in response.

My next frame only gets me four. I chug down half of my beer while gazing across the packed bowling alley. At least it looks like everyone is having fun. The organization even brought in a bunch of players from the Velocity's farm team for the event, which they don't usually do.

Several frames later, I'm on my second beer and only up to thirty-seven points. Nils has three strikes and two spares. Normally, I play a lot better than this... Okay, so I'm not amazing, but I can at least usually break a hundred points in an entire game. I glance down the alley toward Patrick's lane, trying to see his score, but I'm too far away. At this rate, I'm going to get stomped by him, and I'll *never* hear the end of it.

I'm lining up for the next frame when I hear Nils clear his throat from behind me.

"Can I help you?" he asks, motioning to the ball.

"Sure?" I say, unsure of how he's going to help.

He comes to stand behind me and then reaches his arms around me, placing his hands over the top of mine.

The contact is instantly electric. Every inch of my skin immediately ripples into goosebumps, and my mind becomes fuzzy as all of the air is sucked out of the room. What is this feeling?

"You're turning your wrist too far at the last second," Nils says from over my shoulder. He's only an inch or two taller than I am.

I feel like I haven't taken a breath in several minutes, but I must have at some point because I can smell his cologne. It's a subtle but masculine woodsy scent.

"You have to release the ball and end with your hand out like you're going to give a handshake."

I notice how soft his hands are as we go through the motion of the wrist-twist. I'm carefully watching the movement of his pale-but-muscular arms. The hair on them is so light that it nearly disappears against his skin tone.

"Here," he says as we pause with my hand stretched outward, both of us still holding on to the bright pink ball. "This is where you want to release."

"Okay," I somehow manage to squeak out.

He steps back from me, breaking the contact. I didn't realize how tense I was until he moves away. Shaking my head to clear it, I concentrate and follow the steps, releasing the ball as I was instructed. It glides down the lane and directly into the pins, knocking down nine of them.

"Much better," he says with a satisfied smile.

3

MORGAN

The next day, I head into work. I bartend and serve at a local dive bar called Two Bits Pub, a kitschy little place down the road from the Velocity's arena. Bartending there isn't my dream job by any means, but it is something fun and challenging for now.

I've always dreamed of getting a degree and owning my own business someday. What kind of business, I don't know. But I flunked out of college – not because I'm stupid, but I guess I just wasn't ready for the go-to-school-and-get-a-career-and-be-a- responsible-adult phase of my life. I partied too much, studied too little, and got kicked out of the University of Minnesota at the end of my freshman year.

And then, out of the blue, Dad died.

He hadn't been sick, and he wasn't old. He was

simply in the wrong place at the wrong time. He had been in a rougher part of town, picking up a bouquet of flowers for his and Mom's twenty-third anniversary, when he was shot in the back. The bullet went straight through his heart, and he was dead before his body even hit the ground.

The kid who murdered him, only a couple months younger than me, mistook my father for another guy. It was a drug deal gone wrong. And now, the guy is going to sit in jail for the rest of his life to pay for his choice. But my mom, brother, and I will never be able to see my dad again.

It happened during the summer, which is the offseason for Patrick, which meant he was able to come home and be with us as we all grieved. By preseason, he was able to compartmentalize that part of his life into a little box and fully focus back on hockey. I'm not as good at that as him.

Patrick and I have always been super close. When the season started back up, I missed him immensely. So, I packed up and moved in with him in Chicago and have lived here for the last three years.

Ever the resilient one, Mom decided to stay in Minneapolis and throw herself headlong into her career in floral design. She's now one of the top florists in the entire state of Minnesota. She flies down for a lot of Patrick's games, though, or just to visit when she gets bored, so it never feels like she's that far away from us.

My best friend back home, Jade Thomas, is a wedding planner whose business is rapidly growing. As a result, we don't see each other very often except over FaceTime. Brenna is a newer friend, who recently got engaged to one of Pat's teammates, and she introduced me to her friends Carly and John, who are getting married later this month. Other than that, I have a couple regulars at the pub I'll chat with but no one else I'd really call a "friend."

It isn't that I'm antisocial – quite the opposite, in fact. I think I terrify Brenna sometimes with my random bursts of energy and craziness, and I can rally a group of people behind a cause with no problem. I just don't find most people to be engaging or interesting enough for me. I get bored easily, I guess.

That's also why I've never managed to date a guy for more than a couple of months. I get bored with them, they get annoyed, and it doesn't end well.

Having an overprotective older brother doesn't help with my dating prospects either.

I unlock the back door and let myself into the kitchen. The owner of the bar, Steve, is already there, chopping veggies to prepare for the day. He's an eclectic-looking man, with long, silvery hair that reaches mid-back, and he's always wearing a bomber jacket. He reminds me of The Dude from *The Big Lebowski* but with better style.

"Morning," he says to me, a smile in his gravelly voice.

"Hey," I reply with a grin. I head out to the bar area to start my prep work for the day by taking inventory of the syrups and alcohols. Once I've made a list of what I need, I head back into the kitchen.

I set up shop at the cutting board next to Steve and start topping up my stock of simple syrups. This is our comfortable routine, and I savor this time with someone I respect so much.

Although he looks nothing like someone who would be the owner of a popular pub in downtown Chicago, Steve works harder than anyone I know. He's literally poured his blood, sweat, and tears into Two Bits. This place, from what I've been told, was an absolute dump when he bought it ten years ago, but a new visitor would never know that now.

"You know, our boys are looking pretty good this year," he muses over the sound of his knife slicing through green peppers. "I know it's still a little ways out, but you might want to start working on a specialty cocktail for the playoff run."

My hand wavers, and I quickly set down the glass bottle I'm holding. "But Danielle has always done the specialty drinks," I say to him in protest. "She hasn't stopped talking about the Canadian Zamboni-Bomb, and that was two years ago." Her twist on an Irish Car-Bomb wasn't even that good.

"I know," he says, not looking up at me. "But I am sure you're full of good ideas. Plus, I think it's time to give someone else a shot at it." He pushes the mountain of diced green peppers into a bowl. "I know you don't think you can do it, but humble me and try to come up with something anyway?"

I laugh and go back to pouring. "Okay, okay, I'll do it. But if you think I'm the one telling Danielle, then you're a fucking idiot. You know she will be pissed, and I am not about to deal with your stepdaughter's shitty attitude."

He's not her biggest fan, but he has to employ her per the missus at home. Thankfully, Danielle is pretty good at what she does – when she wants to do it – but she isn't happy if she doesn't get her way.

"Fine, I'll take care of Danielle. You start working on a drink," he says. He tosses a piece of pepper at me, hitting me on the cheek. "It better be good!"

IT'S BEEN A SLOW MORNING, so I'm thrilled when I see Brenna walk in the front door around lunchtime. We haven't known each other for very long, but we've quickly become close friends. She used to stop in here a lot more often, but last week she moved out of her place nearby and in with her fiancé, Ryan, in the suburbs.

I start pouring her a beer before she even reaches the bar. "Hey girl," I say to her. "Who should I be expecting?"

"Me, Ry, Matus, and Nils," she answers with a friendly smile. She flicks her thumb over her shoulder to the table in the corner, her long blond hair swinging across her dainty shoulders with the motion. "I think we'll set up shop over there."

"Sure thing," I say, setting her beer on the bar top as I spin around to begin pouring the rest of the guys' drinks. Most of the team frequents Two Bits, due mostly to our close proximity to the arena, so I know their orders by heart. Matus drinks light beer, Nils prefers IPAs, and Ryan will drink anything you set in front of him.

I'm placing the last beer on the bar when the guys walk in the door. They're each freshly showered from morning practice, their various lengths of hair slightly stiff from the frozen outside air. The next home game is tomorrow, followed by a three-game road trip. I don't mind when the team has away games because that means I get the entire condo to myself.

Most people turn their noses up when they hear

I'm in my twenties and live with my older brother, but it works for us. Patrick's income easily covers rent, and he doesn't charge me to live there, but I do most of the chores and errands, including making sure the bills are paid on time. As smart as my brother is, he hasn't figured out that you can set almost every single bill to autopay.

Of course, I'd love to be fully independent and in an apartment on my own, but our arrangement benefits us emotionally too. Dad's death rocked us both, and we grew closer through processing our grief together.

However, he is still my annoying older brother, and road trips with him out of the house for a few days are *always* welcome.

"Thanks, Morgan!" Matus says as he grabs the glass of pisswater – I mean, Bud Light – from the bar. He's the tallest and definitely the most outgoing of these four guys. He is so extroverted that I think he even wears out other extroverts somehow. He says hi to every single restaurant patron as he walks from the bar to the table Brenna has claimed.

My brother is fairly outgoing as well, but both Ryan and Nils are so quiet – especially Nils. I think before our conversation yesterday, I hadn't heard more than ten words cumulatively from him.

The rest of the group greets me, grabs their drinks,

and joins Brenna at the table. I turn around to straighten bottles, but Brenna calls out to me, "Morgan! We actually need you for a sec."

Confused, I glance over to my one other customer, a regular, and make sure he's fine before stepping out from around the bar and walking over to their table.

As I walk, I glance toward the front windows in time to see a flash of red as a Cardinal lands on the sidewalk. Seeing a Cardinal is supposedly a sign that a loved one in heaven is near. I like to believe that it's my Dad showing up to say hello. I smile to myself before sitting at the table with my friends and turning my attention to them.

"As you guys know, we're starting to plan our wedding," Brenna says, looking at all of us. Ryan proposed last week when they moved into their new house. "And, well, I was hoping you'd be my bridesmaid, Morgan."

"And Nils, Matus, will you guys be my groomsmen?" Ryan jumps in after her.

"Of course!" I say enthusiastically. Nils and Matus both agree, and smiles are had all around.

"A toast to the happy couple," Matus says, raising his glass. The rest of the group lift theirs as well. I don't have a drink, so I ball my hand into a fist and clink it with their glasses instead.

"Cheers!" we all say in unison.

Once they've all taken a drink, I ask, "So, who else is in the wedding party?"

"I'm going to have Carly, you, and my co-worker Natalie," Brenna says. "And Ryan will have Patrick, Nils, and Matus."

"When is the big day?" Matus asks, his Slovakian accent heavy.

"Not this summer but the next," Brenna replies. "I don't want to throw something together and have it be lame. I'd rather take my time to plan it out."

"My friend Jade from back home is a wedding planner. I should connect you two," I tell her. "And of course, my mom's a florist, so you already know where your flowers are coming from."

"I'm glad you both have this thing under control," Ryan says with a smirk as he leans back in his seat. "I'll just be over here with the guys, drinking beer if you need anything." Brenna playfully punches his shoulder.

I glance over at my other table across the room. "All right, I gotta get back behind the bar. Anyone need anything?" They all shake their heads, and I head back to my station, a little spring returned to my step.

4

NILS

I needed a relaxing afternoon hanging out with good company after a tough practice this morning. I enjoy sitting back and listening to Brenna's and Ryan's banter, peppered with Matus's exuberant interjections. Brenna mentions something about Ryan's skates smelling so horrible that their entire house stinks after practice. Matus responds with a "That's what she said!" joke in his heavily accented English that makes us all burst into laughter at how absurd it is. He just learned the phrase recently and has been using it whenever possible, even when it doesn't make sense. I think that makes it even funnier.

I'm thankful to have found a loving and supportive hockey family. Between these guys and a couple dudes who are still on the farm team, I've built a pretty supportive group of friends here in the States.

I'm glad to finally feel like I'm fitting in and have found this tight-knit group of friends because my first couple of years here were hard. I've always struggled with my mental health, so when I had a mental breakdown a few seasons ago and didn't have any close friends to support me, it was isolating.

My entire family still lives in Sweden, and experiencing that without them was tough. I don't get to visit them much during the season. My parents came here for Christmas this year because I had a home game the day after. I miss them a lot, as well as my younger siblings, but I know they're all proud of me. They watch as many games as they're able to, even with the time zone differences.

Speaking of zones... I've zoned out on the conversation, but that's all right. I don't always have a ton to add to the conversations. I'm perfectly happy to smile and nod along because I'm just glad to be here.

Out of the corner of my eye, I notice Morgan placing four fresh beers on the edge of the bar for us, so I stand up to grab them.

"I was just gonna come around and bring those over," she says, brushing her dark bangs to one side so they're out of her eyes. She looks a little stressed out, although the bar is not busy at all right now. "Thanks, Nils."

"Not a problem," I tell her with an earnest smile as

I grab two mug handles in each hand and carefully take the drinks back to our table.

Matus and Ryan are talking about some video game they've been playing.

"You do not need an eighty-five-inch television just for gaming," Brenna is saying as I slide into my seat.

"But, babe, the new systems are made for bigger screens," Ryan counters. "You lose all the details if you're playing on a smaller screen."

Brenna looks to me for backup, but I shrug. I don't play video games very often and don't even own any of the newer systems. A lot of the guys on the team are big gamers, though. I'd rather play a physical sport instead of a virtual one.

I glance back at Morgan and watch her moving around the bar. She's picking up various bottles of liquor, staring at them, and putting them down. I'd think she was checking the levels of each to restock, but she isn't grabbing new bottles of anything. I decide to go sit at the bar and see what's on her mind.

"Hey," I say as I sit down, grabbing a drink napkin before setting down my beer.

"Hey. You need something?" she asks.

"No." I look over my shoulder toward our group of friends. My shoulder-length hair is still damp from my shower earlier, and it gets in my face. I should have put it into a ponytail. "They're talking about video games."

She rolls her eyes. "They got Patrick hooked on some futuristic, shoot-em-up, space game a few weeks ago. He stayed up until like four the other night playing online with them."

"I guess you don't play much either?"

"Definitely not," she says with a laugh. Her smile lights up her entire face, I notice. Suddenly, she claps her hands together excitedly. "Hey! You can be my guinea pig!"

I furrow my brow, confused by her words. English isn't my first language, and sometimes I forget words or use them wrong. "Guinea pig? Isn't that a little rodent pet?"

She lets out a full-bellied laugh, head thrown back – the kind that makes you do it too. You can't help it because it's contagious. "Yes," she finally says through lingering giggles. "But it's also an expression because guinea pigs were used for product testing a long time ago, for makeup and medicine and things. You can be my test subject."

"Before I agree, what exactly will I be testing?" I ask skeptically.

One hand on her hip, she says, "My boss asked me to come up with my own original cocktail for the Velocity's playoff run since it looks like you'll make it in. I need to try out some different ideas, and I have to make sure they don't suck." She smiles at me, her nose crinkled. Damn, she's cute. "Would you be willing to taste-test for me?"

I shrug but match her smile. Free booze sounds good to me. "Sure, why not?"

She fist-pumps into the air. "Yes! Thank you, thank you, thank you!"

"Good lord, what did you do to her, Nils?" says a voice from behind me. I swivel around to see Brenna standing there, a bemused expression on her face.

"Nothing," I say matter-of-factly.

"He agreed to try some new mixed drink ideas I have," Morgan says to her friend, who is now seated next to me at the bar. "Will you try them too, Brenna?"

"Sure," Brenna replies. "Just tell me when and where. And make sure I have a designated driver. You know I'm a total lightweight."

Morgan winks at Brenna. "Can do."

"Well, we are getting ready to leave," Brenna says. She reaches into her large purse that has absolutely seen better days, digging briefly before pulling out an envelope and handing it to Morgan. "Carly and John asked me to give this to you since they didn't have your address. It's the invitation to their wedding in a couple weeks for you and Patrick."

"Awesome, thanks!"

"Not a problem. See you all later," Brenna says as she hops off the barstool and meets Ryan at the end of the table. Apparently, Matus is leaving too because the three of them wave and bid their goodbyes to Morgan and I before heading out the door.

"When would you be free to get together to try out these drinks?" Morgan asks, bringing my focus back to her.

"Whenever." I shrug.

She rolls her eyes at me. "So vague. Be more specific, please."

"Fine," I say back. "Tonight?"

She looks a little stunned but quickly recovers. "That's fine. I get off at five. What's your address?"

"I never said I was hosting."

"You're the one who suggested tonight," she quips. Her hand is still on her hip, and I notice how it accentuates the notch of her slim waist. "If you want to do a different day, I'll host it, but since I don't even get out of work until five and would still need to clean because god knows Patrick doesn't—"

"Okay, fine. You can come to my house." I give her my address, and she plugs it into her phone as I set cash on the bar top for my tab. "See you tonight."

My house is spotless, and a spread of various veggies, cheeses, and fruit is prepped when Morgan finally shows up at almost seven. Since I wasn't sure what non-alcoholic ingredients she may need for her drink recipes, I tried to have a bit of everything ready to go. Plus, I thought we'd need snacks.

"Sorry I'm late! I had to pick up booze!" she says as she kicks her tennis shoes off onto the mat next to the front door. I help her carry one of the reusable bags into the kitchen.

"This is a nice place," she says, looking around my kitchen. It is a bit more "rustic charm" than would be my normal style, but I keep it pretty minimal. I don't own a lot of stuff, and the things I do own are simple and clean.

"Wow, you certainly didn't miss a single detail, did you?" she says to me, audibly impressed as she examines the bowls of ingredients on the center island. I just smile at her as I grab a piece of knäckebröd, my favorite type of cracker from back home, and lean back against the counter. She starts to pull bottles of alcohol out of the bags.

"So, what's the purpose of you making drinks again?" I ask.

"My boss thinks we're going to make it into the playoffs, which he's probably right with the way this season has been going. So, he wants ideas for special drinks to offer during the playoff run. It's a marketing gimmick, really, but Steve usually only lets his stepdaughter come up with cool new drinks. Him giving me a shot will piss off Danielle. Therefore, I need to make something extra amazing."

I've been watching her hands deftly move across the island's top as she talks, pouring carefully measured liquids into glasses. Her fingernails are painted black like always. She wastes no time getting the first drink into my hand.

"A rum and Coke?" I ask.

"This one is a warmup." She grins at me, holding a glass in her hand as well. She comes around the island to clink her glass against mine. "To creating something amazing together. Cheers."

"Cheers," I echo, my eyes locked with hers over the rim of our glasses. Here goes nothing.

5

MORGAN

Nils carefully watches me start working on my first drink idea: a brandy cocktail. I'm glad he was willing to be my guinea pig for this. I am so nervous about Danielle being pissed at me, so the sooner I can create the perfect drink, the better.

He looks so calm and relaxed right now, leaning against the counter with the rum and Coke in hand. It's quite different from how I see him on game days. At games, he seems calm, but anyone can tell he is radiating with nervous, electric energy. The more time I spend with him, the more I get the impression that he isn't nearly as calm on the inside as he portrays himself to be.

I finish mixing the drink and set the glass on the edge of the countertop for him. "First up."

He takes the glass in his free hand, holding it up to

examine it. "You are going to work on the presentation, right?"

"Wow, bustin' my balls already," I say with snark. "Yes, I will. Today is about taste, not presentation."

He takes a small sip of it and immediately looks disgusted. "Why does this taste like something I would use to clean the toilet?"

I am laughing so hard I'm doubled over, and I hear him start to chuckle too. The sound echoes off the walls, filling the room with a warm, beautiful chorus.

After a few moments of belly laughs, I finally pull myself together and straighten up. The laughter is still making its way through him. His face is flushed, and his eyes are glowing under his wavy blond hair. *Oh.*

A flash of desire cuts through me. *What the hell?* I quickly squash it down.

"I'm sorry," I say, hoping he thinks the pink in my cheeks is only from cracking up and not from the lust for him that I just felt. "Apparently, that one is no good. I'm experimenting with different flavors than you'd normally pair together."

"You're trying to kill me," he scoffs, then smiles to let me know he's joking. "I hope you are not offended if I dump this one out."

"Go for it," I tell him with a flick of my wrist. I'm already working on the next drink physically but trying to get my brain back on task as well.

Twenty minutes and six drinks later, I think we are finally getting somewhere. Nils has taken two sips out of his current drink instead of just one. I'll count that as progress.

"How long have you been bartending?" he asks me.

"A year or so." I pour raspberry liqueur into the shaker. "I got a job at Two Bits right after moving to Chicago, but I didn't start bartending right away."

"How long have you lived here?"

"It'll be three years this summer," I reply. "I moved in with Patrick after our dad died."

"Oh, uh, I'm so sorry," he says quickly, his face showing regret in having asked.

"It's okay. I don't mind talking about it." I pick up the shaker and start rattling it over my shoulder. After a few seconds, I set it on the counter. "It's been good for both Pat and me. I had just failed out of college, and he was a brand-new captain, dealing with the murder of our father. We needed each other."

Nils looks down at the drink in his hand, visibly tossing my matter-of-fact words around in his head. He takes a third sip from the glass, carefully choosing his next words. "You and your brother are very close."

"Yeah, I'd say so." I separate the shaker glasses and

place the strainer against it. "He's so damn restrictive, but I know he's trying to do the job that Dad isn't here to do." I pause and fill the rocks glass in front of me for him. "It doesn't mean it's right, but I can't really fault him for trying to fill Dad's shoes in my life, you know? I know he loves me, and this is his way of showing it."

Nils moves away from the counter he's been leaning against and comes to the island, resting his elbows on it. His eyes are green, with bits of gold in them, I notice for the first time, and he has a light splattering of freckles across his nose. He's so close to me that I swear I feel the air crackle between us. "How is he overprotective of you?"

I slide Nils the seventh drink. He grasps it in his hand, but his eyes are focused on me, curious.

"I mean, you already know. None of you guys on the team can even *look* at me, let alone consider dating me." My dating life has been absolutely non-existent since I've moved to Chicago, but I won't be telling Nils that. Nor will I tell him that the only action I've gotten in the last three years has been from my vibrator.

He has a peculiar look on his face, and my arms are instantly covered in goosebumps. What is going through his head? He stands up straight, the same weird look still on his face. "Do you like to go fast, Morgan?"

I feel one of my eyebrows cock upwards. "Yes? I think? What kind of a question is that?"

"Let me show you something." Forgetting the drinks on the counter, he grabs one of my hands and quite literally pulls me out of the kitchen toward the door heading outside.

"Nils! I'm not wearing shoes or a coat!" I manage to get him to stop long enough to slide on my shoes before he's dragging me out the door, stumbling into the February night.

He's grinning as he leads me into a building behind his house. I have never seen him so excited, except for maybe when he scores a goal.

We emerge into a parking garage, and he leads me over to a sleek, black motorcycle.

"Is this yours?" I ask him.

He nods. "This is my pride and joy." We stare at it in silence for a second, before he turns to face me. "Want to go for a ride?"

"Are you crazy!? It's the middle of February!"

"Morgan, *det finns inget dåligt väder, bara dåliga kläder,*" he says. "'There's no bad weather, only bad clothing'. But I have a jacket you can borrow."

"Okay, but it's dark, and you've been drinking."

"Come on. The bike has headlights, and I've only had a couple sips over the course of several hours. We will be fine."

"I still don't think it's a good idea," I reply, crossing my arms over my chest for warmth. I can see my breath curling into the air between us.

"Is that Morgan talking, or is it Patrick?"

Something about that question grinds me the wrong way, but it also ignites something within me as well. Maybe it's a bit of rebelliousness against my older brother, who isn't here to watch over me, and a bit of excitement in doing something new with someone I'm having a good time with.

I cave. "Okay. Let's do it."

Nils hands me a black Velocity sweatshirt. My hands are shaking slightly as I pull it on over my head. I'm not entirely sure if I'm shaking because I'm nervous that I'm about to ride on a motorcycle for the first time or because the sweatshirt smells like him.

Maybe it's both. Yeah, that's probably it.

He passes me a helmet, and I quickly put it on as he pops another over his head. I try to secure the chin strap on mine, but my fingers fumble with it. Immediately, he takes over, his fingers inches from my face. Gently brushing my chin and neck as he works the strap with dexterity, he secures the helmet onto my head with ease.

"Is that too tight?" he asks me, his voice muffled by the foam inside the helmet. I shake my head no, and he deftly gets his chin strap in place before tossing me a pair of riding gloves.

"I'm going to get on first, and then you place your foot on this peg to get on behind me," he says.

I can't see anything except his gold-flecked eyes in the opening of his helmet and a little bit of his blond hair sticking out of the bottom of it. I nod in reply and watch as he gracefully swings a leg over the bike, settling onto the dip of the seat.

"Whenever you're ready, Morgan," he shouts to me, the smile in his voice not lost. I place a foot on the peg and grab onto his shoulders, and with a small hop to boost myself, I manage to swing my leg over the back of the bike, planting myself onto the seat behind him. I swear I can already feel the bike's power, and a shiver passes down my spine.

Nils turns his head to the side, which is as close as we can get to eye contact in this position. "Are you good?"

"Yeah, I think so," I yell back, making sure my feet are securely on the pegs. He scoots back on his seat a little, and I feel the warmth of his body as he settles in between my thighs. "Wait, where do I put my hands?"

"Wrap them around me, like this." He grabs my wrists and wraps my arms around his waist. I link my fingers together over his abdomen. Even through his leather jacket and my gloves, I can feel the movement of his stomach as he breathes.

I shift my weight, leaning a little less against him. "I'm afraid I'm going to crush you."

"You're not going to crush me. Be sure to hold on tight, and if you need me to stop, hit my leg so I know."

The bike revs to life beneath us, purring in a way only something with that much horsepower can. He flips up the kickstand with his foot, and we take off, rolling down the driveway and onto the street. At the stop sign at the end of his block, he checks in with a questioning thumbs up. I give him a confident thumbs up, and he turns back to the road, pulling down the visor on his helmet.

The bike lurches forward, and I'm not holding on anywhere near well enough for the sudden change in motion. I clutch onto him much more tightly as we accelerate down the road toward the highway, terrified and curious and amazed.

He hits the on-ramp for I-90, and I feel the acceleration of the bike as he gets up to speed, merging seamlessly into the busy evening traffic. The wind whips around us, and I'm thankful Nils let me borrow a sweatshirt for the ride. It's cold, but he's blocking most of the wind for me.

I'm hyperaware of our proximity as I pull myself a

little closer to him for stability. Even with bumpy pavement and rushing wind, I can still feel his breathing beneath me. It's smooth and steady, and I shouldn't be surprised because that's typical Nils – he's always so calm, cool, and collected.

Meanwhile, my excited heart is traveling even faster than we are. The apprehension I once held has been replaced by wonder, amazement, and pure adrenaline coursing through me. I watch the trees and houses and sound walls all blur as we zip past. Nils slows and navigates us off the ramp then onto the freeway again, and we barrel back toward the downtown Chicago skyline.

We're going fast on the crowded highway, riding on a motorcycle inches from potential disaster, but with Nils, I feel safe. I feel alive. I feel free.

The sun's last rays stretch across the sky, trying to reach us between buildings and clouds while painting a glorious sunset over the glass and metal of the city. There's something about the way the sky kisses the horizon that is absolutely sublime.

He exits the freeway and pulls off into a parking lot. Once we're stopped, he flips down the kickstand and pulls up his visor. "How is it so far?"

I flip up my visor too. "It's *awesome*," I gush. I see the corner of his eye crinkle with a smile.

"Let's get back out there, then," he says, pushing his visor back down and pulling up the kickstand. I settle into position against him, my awareness of how close we are once again brought to the forefront of my mind. I try not to think about how I'm pressed up against a hot guy's back, my hands on his abs, my thighs squeezing his sides for support... damn it.

Thankfully, the scenic ride once again distracts me. The sun has almost entirely disappeared below the horizon as we turn around and head toward his house. I'm sure I'm wide-eyed, watching the city under the magic and wonder of twilight.

Traffic is finally thinning out as we near Nils's house. He changes lanes and lays into the throttle, zooming past car after car as we hurtle down the highway. We pass under streetlights that dance across the road like a well-choreographed ballet.

When we pull onto his street, he lets off the gas, coasting into the garage before slowing to a stop in his designated spot. He climbs off first and offers me his hand to help me. As I place my palm into his, my pulse spikes. It can't be safe for my heart to be beating this fast.

Nils has taken off his helmet, his long hair haphazard. I remove my own and our eyes finally meet. We're both wearing grins a mile wide.

"That was fucking *amazing*," I practically yell in my excitement. Nils grabs my helmet and sets both of them on the back of the bike. He pulls off his gloves and puts them on the bike seat with the helmets, and I do the same with mine.

"I've never seen you look so happy," he says. My smile falters slightly. "No, that's not a bad thing. You look thrilled, and I love that you enjoyed it."

"Well, thank you so much for that incredible experience," I enthuse. "I can't believe how much power that thing has… and yet it felt so smooth and… wow. I am overwhelmed in a good way, Nils. Thank you. You didn't have to do that for me."

"Of course I did. It was my pleasure." He rakes a hand through his hair, but it doesn't help put any of it back into place.

I feel a smile spread across my lips. "Here, let me help." I reach up and run my hands through his golden hair, untangling the strands to make it look more trendy-windswept than hit-by-a-tornado.

Satisfied with my handiwork, my hands return to my sides, but my feet refuse to move. We're standing very close together – close enough for me to see his throat bob, despite his beard partially obscuring it.

"I wonder what it would feel like to have my hands in your hair," he muses, voice low. Slowly, his right hand rises to the side of my face as he tucks a piece behind my ear.

It's a gentle act that instantly sends my brain to a filthy place, and he must know it. Under his hungry gaze, a shiver moves all the way down my spine, and I have to suppress a moan.

"I didn't think it was possible for you to be so quiet, Morgan."

"And I didn't think it was possible for you to be so..." I trail off.

"So what?" he challenges.

I turn my head and am face-to-face with him. His evergreen eyes search my face, lingering on my lips, and I clench my thighs together. "So not what I expected," I finally say.

"How so?"

"Until today, I only knew you as shy and quiet. But you seem so sure of yourself now. So... in control."

A throaty groan escapes him. Suddenly, his lips crush against mine. My body responds to the contact and melts into his, pulling him closer as our mouths connect over and over. Our kisses are greedy and filled with electric desire. His beard lightly scratches the sensitive skin of my face, and I begin to feel warmth low in my belly. I want him to touch me, to explore every inch of me with this mouth and those hands.

Somehow, I manage to get enough blood to my brain to realize that I'm kissing a hockey player. I do *not* kiss hockey players. Especially not hockey players that are on Patrick's team. Who the hell am I? I'm not like this with guys – ever. But the physical connection between Nils and I... I've never felt anything like it before.

Or maybe I'm just horny.

I manage to pull away from him and nearly whimper out loud from the sudden disconnect. I'm wide-eyed; he's smirking.

"Well, that was unexpected," he says in a matter-of-fact tone in that glorious accent, and damn if my body doesn't respond to it. Even though we're in the winter air, my body is steaming hot and screaming at me with need.

"I-I have to get going," I tell him hastily. I grab the car key out of my pocket and step back from him. If he's disappointed, I can't tell. "Thank you again for the ride tonight."

"Do you need your stuff?" he asks.

I shake my head. I didn't bring a purse with me, and I don't care about the booze. I have to get out of here before I lose what little restraint I currently have. "Don't worry about it."

"Okay," he says without hesitation. I still can't tell what he's thinking, but at this point, it's taking all of my focus to walk away from him right now. I quickly climb into my car, and I awkwardly wave goodbye as I haul ass down the street and away from him.

What the hell was that? I mentally reprimand myself. I do not, under any circumstances, make out with hockey players. To do so with one of Patrick's teammates? I must have a death wish. If he finds out...

As I drive, I try to talk myself down. Nils is a man of few words, after all. I don't think he's the kind of guy to kiss and tell in the locker room. Especially if he knows what's good for him. Hopefully, we can pretend this never happened.

6

NILS

As usual, I'm the first one to the practice rink the next morning. Getting here early is my thing. I enjoy the peace and quiet as I walk through the small arena, flicking the light switches and hearing the old incandescent bulbs hum as they warm up. The sound of my shoes slapping the concrete floor is satisfying, echoing off cinderblock and steel walls. I enjoy getting dressed in the locker room alone, sitting on the wooden bench with its peeling red paint as I pull my skates on and methodically lace them up, appreciating the solitude. And even more than all of that, I love being the first to hit fresh ice.

When I get out there, I usually do a few leisurely laps around the very edge of the rink. The way my skates' blades cut through the clean surface helps wake me up. Then, I do sprints back and forth across the full length of the rink as fast as I can go.

Some people choose to do yoga or meditation or go to church, but racing across untouched ice is my spiritual experience. There is nothing that an early morning skate can't fix.

Well, almost nothing.

I shouldn't have kissed Morgan. There are a few people in my life who are off-limits, and she's one of them. I have seen the way Patrick freaks out on anyone who even looks at her.

It's a shame, though, because she's lovely to look at. Her jet-black hair perfectly frames her angular face and accentuates her gold-colored eyes. She has her own unique sense of style that is comfortable and yet doesn't look odd or out of place. Plus, her body is insane.

Her exhilaration after getting off the bike was so enticing. Probably because that elation is the same feeling I have every time I ride. I think she loved it just as much as I do.

Her lips were soft, begging for me to kiss them endlessly. I knew she was into it too by the way her body responded to my kiss. The way she pressed up against me, like any space between us was too much, is addicting. It made me want even more of her. That one searing kiss will keep me awake for the rest of my life. It'll never be enough.

Why does she have to be Patrick's sister?

Focus.

I rush across the ice at breakneck speed, as fast as my legs and the blades will carry me, to outrun those thoughts. When I reach the end of the rink, I slam on the brakes, showering bits of ice all over the glass wall behind the net, mere inches from the boards.

"Damn, Nils, are you trying to break the fastest skater record?" Ryan's voice yells at me from across the rink, pulling me out of my thoughts and into reality. I hear him step onto the ice and we glide toward each other.

"Yeah, something like that," I reply as casual as I can.

"Well, if you get invited to the All-Star Game next year, I'm betting on you," he says as I plop down on the center line to do a few stretches.

"Thanks," I say absently, my mind still preoccupied by Morgan. Apparently, I can't just skate her out of my thoughts like I had hoped to do.

Patrick would kill both of us if he knew I put the moves on his little sister, so I'm never going to tell him or anyone else what happened. And I'll just have to make sure it never happens again.

"Are you going to Two Bits after practice?" Patrick asks as he grabs his duffel bag from his locker stall.

"Uh..." I trail off, my brain panicking. "No, not today."

"Why not?" Ryan jumps in. His locker is in-between mine and Patrick's. "Plenty of time to grab a beer before the road trip."

I wrack my brain for a lie. "I haven't packed yet."

Patrick and Ryan both stare at me like I've grown a third arm. "Seriously?" Ryan asks in an incredulous tone. "You are always repacked and ready to go the day after we get back from a trip."

Anxiously, I rub the back of my neck. "I know, I just... got busy. I'll catch you later." I grab my bag and head out of the locker room, trying to ignore the feeling of their eyes on my back.

I'm not ready to see Morgan again quite yet. If things are awkward between us, I'd rather them be awkward without Patrick there to witness it.

I'm almost to my car in the team parking lot when Matus calls out to me. He has his typical devilish grin on his face.

"What are you doing for the next couple hours?" he asks, jogging across the lot to catch up. It doesn't take any time at all with how long his legs are compared to mine. He's easily two hundred cm tall. Or six-foot-seven for the strange people who don't use the metric system.

"I'm packing," I say with a bit more confidence in the lie this time, my hand resting on the door handle of my car. "Why?"

A questioning expression briefly crosses his face before he holds up two paper tickets. "The girl I hooked up with last night works at one of the fully nude strip clubs here in town. Want to go before we leave?"

"Dude, it's noon on a Monday." I chuckle.

"Come on, man." He waves the tickets in front of my face, teasing me. "VIP. You know you want to go see some titties."

Matus can be such a bad influence, but also such a good time. I sigh. I know I won't have any trouble picking up one of the dancers for a few hours of fun. The girls at this club are easy.

I guess if I can't skate Morgan out of my head, maybe I can fuck her out of it instead. "All right, let's go."

7

MORGAN

I don't hear from Nils before the team heads out on a road trip, but I didn't expect to either. We both got caught up in the moment. I'm attracted to the guy, sure, because he's hot as hell. The kiss was incredible. I can't stop thinking about the feeling of his lips on mine. I wonder if he's been thinking about it too. Probably not.

It needs to not be a big deal to me.

The condo is quiet without Patrick here. I'd never admit it to him, but I do enjoy his company, even with him being my annoying, messy, bossy older brother. The entire space just doesn't feel as homey without his laughter following me as I take care of the pile of dirty dishes he left on the counter for the millionth time.

Thankfully, I have a video chat scheduled with Jade before I head into work. I throw the top layer of my hair into an elastic to pull it back from my face and settle on top of the poofy grey comforter on my bed with my laptop and a mug of coffee.

My best friend's smile pops onto the screen, sitting at her desk in her beautifully decorated living room. She's wearing a full face of perfect makeup that highlights her gorgeous dark skin. She looks chic in a deep purple blazer with a white shirt underneath.

"Good morning!" she beams. She's so much more of a morning person than I am.

"Good morning, yourself," I reply, taking a drink of coffee and setting the mug back onto my nightstand. "You're awfully cheery today."

"And you're awfully grumpy," she quips, fussing with one of her shoulder-length locs. "What's going on with you?"

I sigh. She has always been able to see right through me. "It's a guy."

"That much was obvious."

I stick my tongue out at her. "His name is Nils, and, well, he's on the team."

She gasps and gets super-close to the camera on her side, making her face huge on my screen. "Nils Larsson? Oh my god, Morgan. You didn't sleep with him, did you?"

"No! Jesus, Jade, you know my rule: no fucking

hockey players." Waving my hand in the air, I then say, "But we did kiss."

She clicks her tongue in response.

I narrow my eyes at her. "Look, it isn't a big deal, all right? It was one kiss. That's it."

"You know Patrick will still murder the poor guy."

"Of course he *would* if he ever found out, which *he will not*." Jade has always proven to be someone I can trust with all my secrets, so this is just another to add to the vault. "This guy is a super introvert. Before the other day, I think I'd only ever heard him say a handful of sentences. He'll keep quiet." *I hope.*

She sits back in her chair, twirling a ballpoint pen between her fingers. "Well, I'm glad you finally got a little action, but I still think you need to have a conversation with Patrick about giving you some space to date."

"I know I should, but you know how hard-headed he is," I say with a sigh. I take another sip of coffee as I contemplate. "I know why he's doing it. He's trying to be what he thinks I need since Dad isn't here. But having some room to breathe would be nice. I'm not a kid anymore."

"I bet," she agrees, chewing lightly on the end of her pen. "Just be careful, okay? I don't want you to get hurt."

"Yeah, yeah, I know. Anyway, what's new with you?"

"New day, same hustle," she says. "Still trying to get more couples to book with me."

"Did Brenna and Ryan contact you? I told her to."

Jade's smile is wide. "She did! I'm really excited to plan their wedding. Thanks for referring your Velocity friends to me."

"Of course," I reply. "I just wish I had more friends getting married so I could bully them all into using your services."

"Maybe someday soon I'll be planning your wedding," she says as she wiggles her eyebrows. "Planning another hockey wedding would be huge for my career."

"I know I've said I would do anything for you, but marrying a hockey player just so you can plan the wedding and get tons of PR from it is where I draw the line."

I show up to work at my normal time to discover Danielle is there. It's her day off, so I'm not sure why she's sitting at the bar, considering she avoids Two Bits like the plague when she isn't scheduled to work.

"Hey, Danielle," I greet her as I toss my purse in the cubby under the bar.

"Don't '*Hey, Danielle*' me," she sneers as I approach her. "If you really think you're going to be doing the specialty cocktail for playoffs, then you're sadly mistaken."

I roll my eyes so hard they nearly fall out of my head. Of course she's here because of the cocktail. I should have known. "If you have a problem with it, you'll need to take it up with your stepfather."

She laughs, and my hatred for her grows even more. Good thing the bar is separating us because I might strangle her if I get close enough.

"Oh, trust me, I already have. He told me that *of course* I can still make a cocktail, and he'll try both of our creations and decide which one is best." Her eyes are filled with disdain. "Of course, we both know whose he will like better."

"Yeah, okay." I turn my back to her and start taking inventory. "You know, maybe if you were nicer to me, I'd actually consider putting in a good word for you with Patrick." It's a poorly kept secret that she's been trying to get in my brother's pants. *Gross*. I know it's a cheap shot to use as leverage, but I'm annoyed and don't care if I'm being childish.

"You seriously think I need your help? Your charity? As if, Morgan." She gets up off the bar stool and zips her coat. "I don't need your help, and honestly, Steve doesn't really either. You know he only keeps you around here because your brother is famous, right?"

I'm glad my back is turned to her because those words cut me. I try to keep my life as normal as possible. I work hard for what I have, and I try even harder not to ride Patrick's coattails. It sounds like a lie since we live together and I don't pay rent, but it's true. He knows I'm working hard to better myself and figure out what I want to do. I also volunteer frequently with the Velocity, visiting children's hospitals, helping organize fundraisers, and other duties for the organization, on top of working full time at Two Bits.

But there is no use in arguing these points with someone who has already made up their mind about me.

"Whatever you say, Danielle," I say softly over my shoulder. She's already left, but unfortunately, her words remain.

8

NILS

The horn blares through the arena, signaling the end of the second period. It's the second game of the road trip, and we're down three-to-one against Boston. Despite the rowdy crowd's energy, the opponents have been fast and tough, and we haven't been able to get pucks in the net.

I follow the team through the tunnel to our locker room, tapping the hands of several young Velocity fans as we lumber past them. I pass my gloves to the equipment manager outside of the locker room before going in. I sit in my assigned stall, and Matus drops heavily into the one next to me.

"Mother fuckers," he says to no one. That's it. No context, just a simple statement. I shrug in halfhearted agreement.

I grab the water bottle from under my seat and

take a big drink from it. Coach Mike has been keeping us with our normal lines so far tonight, but he will probably switch things up in the third to try to make some goals happen. I don't love it when our lines go through the blender mid-game. But I also understand that sometimes, it is necessary. It keeps us on our toes and keeps the other team on theirs.

"Did you see the absolute rack on that blond babe in the second row behind our net?" Matus asks me. "Almost turned over the puck when I saw those jugs."

"You are ridiculous," the guy on the other side of Matus says. It's Alexei Kalinin, a Russian-born Canadian and one of our centers. He and I are from the same draft class, although I was drafted a couple rounds ahead of him. "Do you ever stop thinking about boobs?"

"No." Matus shrugs. Alexei shakes his head in mild disgust, and I chuckle.

"Hey, man, she does have a great rack," our goalie, Landon Jacobi, says from his stall across the room. He mimes sticking his face in between a set of huge boobs to the laughter of the locker room. "Impossible not to notice those tits."

"See, Landon agrees with me," Matus says to Alexei. "Hey, Landon, want to place a bet? Twenty dollars says I bag her tonight."

"Make it fifty and I'm in," Landon replies with a

huge grin. A couple of the other guys whoop and yell out their own bets. We wouldn't normally have time for a one-night stand after an away game. Most days, we leave from a game straight to the airport for our next destination. But we aren't leaving until tomorrow afternoon for our game with Minnesota the day after that. Matus very well could win this bet.

Whenever there's enough time without practice, travel, or a game, a lot of the guys will try to squeeze something in. Some of them have side chicks in various cities, some of them swipe through Tinder between periods to see who they can meet up with, and some just scope out girls in the stands and hope they're waiting around outside the doors after the game, like some puck bunnies do.

More often than not, I hook up while on the road. It's just how life is in the NHL. Eat, sleep, hockey, fuck, repeat. I like road chicks because there are fewer expectations. If they know hockey, then they know we're just in town for the game and don't usually try to make a thing out of it. They seem to understand the "one" in "one-night stand" better than local girls.

The coaches come into the locker room, and we all quickly quiet down. I mentally shake off the last few minutes. Time to get our heads back in the game and try to pull out a win.

———

WELL, we give up an empty-net goal, ending the game with a four-to-one loss. Throwing the lines into the blender didn't work this time. I played for a while on Alexei's line instead of with Ryan and Patrick, which threw me off my groove. Landon played a great game for us, making several spectacular saves that will probably be on all the highlight reels tonight. But we got outplayed. It happens. We can't win them all, I suppose.

I barely have my pads off before Matus is dressed and rushing out of the locker room, presumably to go find the woman with the huge tits. I don't blame him. I looked for her in the third period during a TV timeout. Holy hell, they *were* huge.

Almost too big, honestly.

Morgan's are perfect, though.

I shake my head. *What the fuck, Nils? Get it together.* I can't be thinking about Patrick's sister like that.

Speaking of...

I glance over at Patrick. He's sitting in his stall a few down from mine, still fully dressed minus his gloves and helmet. His head is between his hands, and he's staring at the floor, deep in thought. This is normal behavior for him, though. He's always the last one out of the locker room after a loss. He might be haunted by even more demons than I am.

He must feel me looking his way because he raises his head and we lock eyes. He furrows his brow, his face filling with concern as he mouths, *You okay?* I give him a small thumbs up and he smiles slightly before glancing away from me, the concern on his face replaced by age and worry once more.

With a sigh, I head for the showers and am met by Landon, who is walking back to the locker room. The towel around his waist is barely hanging on. It apparently wasn't used to capture any water from the shower. Landon's dark brown skin is still dripping wet.

"Larsson, did Horvath already leave?" he asks me.

"Yeah."

"Fuck, I better hurry, then." He drips water all over the floor. "Don't want him claiming he landed that chick and have it be someone else, like he tried on us last time." He thunders past me toward his locker.

I shower leisurely, letting the hot water cascade across my sore muscles. I'm in no rush to get back to the hotel, but I also don't feel like going out either. Banging someone random just isn't very appealing to me tonight.

Maybe I should text Morgan, I think to myself as I run the bar of soap across my chest, enjoying the feel of the white lather on my skin. Instantly, I squash that idea. I shouldn't text her. We got carried away the other day. If anything, I need to quit thinking about her. Besides, if she wanted to talk to me, she probably would have reached out by now.

Wow, I didn't realize how frustrated I am, but it's caused me to scrub a bit too hard, making my skin angry and red. I set the bar of soap down and continue washing up.

When I exit the showers, it's only myself and Patrick left in the locker room. He's standing near my stall, buttoning his dress shirt. He waits until I've got my boxer-briefs on before initiating conversation.

"Hey, Nils, it's been a while since we've connected, so I wanted to check in and see how you're doing." He doesn't have to expand any further because I know he's asking about my mental health.

"I'm doing okay," I reply mostly in truth as I step into my suit pants.

He finishes with his shirt, and our eyes meet. The concern is back on his face. "Is there anything myself or the team can do to support you?"

"Nah." I button and zip my pants. "I appreciate it. I'm good right now, though." *Except that I can't stop thinking about your little sister.*

"Okay, cool," he says. "I care about you, and I'll continue to be here, not just as your captain but also as your friend."

You wouldn't be my friend if you knew the erotic fantasies that I've been whacking off to every night for the past several days.

Fuck. Maybe I should go out tonight just so I don't sit at the hotel and sulk over someone I can't have.

"Thanks, man. I appreciate it." We clasp hands, and he pulls me into a dude hug, my bare chest bumping lightly against his clothed body in a manly display of caring and kindness.

He lets me get back to dressing, fiddling on his phone until I'm ready to leave. As we walk out, he hits the lights and closes the door behind us.

9

MORGAN

I decide to have a few of the Velocity women over to my place for a viewing party of the third game of the road trip. They're playing our biggest threat for the playoffs, my hometown team, the Minnesota Winter. The Velocity are currently neck-and-neck with the Winter for the top of the league in points, and this is their last time facing each other in the regular season, so it's a high-stakes game.

My Mom decided to come down for the party, which I am so excited about. It's been a few weeks since she's been here, and I could really use her positive energy in my life right now.

She also brought Jade, and they have been here all day helping cook, clean, and prep for the party tonight. I'm thankful for the help. Patrick left his bathroom an absolute disgusting mess before he left, and I've been too much of a mess myself to find the energy to clean it, along with the rest of the house.

With Mom setting off a nuclear bomb of bleach in Pat's bathroom, Jade and I are finally alone in the kitchen. She's been giving me the *I'm worried about you* side-eye ever since she got here.

"Morgs... what's going on?" she finally asks from across the island when she's certain Mom can't hear. I stop stirring the cake batter and set the spoon down with a sigh. It was fully mixed a long time ago, but I was taking my frustration out on it.

"I haven't heard from Nils at all since we kissed," I say.

"You never care if a guy texts you or not," she replies. "Why are you so bothered by him?"

Casting my eyes down to the floor, I let my mind wander out loud. "I barely even knew Nils before the other night. But once we started talking, we had this connection. I felt like I could talk to him for hours. And I know he felt the same way."

"And you're positive you aren't just super horny?" she asks, jeering me.

I playfully throw the empty box of cake mix at her. "Of course I'm fucking horny. I've been on an involuntary sabbatical, unlike *someone* I know." I've been living vicariously through my best friend's sexcapades and a

Costco-sized supply of AA batteries for my vibrator. Desperate times require desperate measures.

"All right, all right. But what is it about this guy that has you so hung up?" She crosses the kitchen with her glass of wine to stand next to me at the counter. Her familiar vanilla and cocoa butter scent is comforting.

I sigh. "You know that I can be a bit of a cold-hearted bitch, right?" She starts to snicker, and I shush her. "Well... Nils made me *feel* something."

"Welcome to the club of people who actually have emotions!" she says with a teasing laugh before she wraps her arm around my shoulder in a side-hug. "Did you ever think about reaching out to him first?"

"Of course I did. But you're forgetting my number one rule."

"Don't fuck hockey players," we say in unison.

"Yes, I know." Jade returns her arm to her side. "I never said you had to fuck him or date him or anything like that. Just talk to him. That's all."

"Talk to who?" Mom asks as she comes into the room. Jade hides a half-smile behind her wine glass, leaving me to cover for us.

"Patrick," I say quickly, grabbing the bowl of cake batter. "About keeping his damn bathroom clean. Hey, can you grab me that box? I need the directions."

Mom tears off her rubber gloves and deposits them

into the trash before grabbing the box on the floor for me. When her back is turned, I glare at Jade. She just smirks in return.

"I swear, you'd think that boy was raised in a barn," Mom says as she hands the box to me. She grabs her coffee from the counter. "And I know he wasn't because I was there. They move out and lose everything you drilled into them. Honestly, it amazes me that you haven't killed him yet."

"Oh, trust me, I've considered it," I reply, turning on the oven. The doorbell rings and I glance at my watch. "Shoot, it's six already. Mom, can you get the door?"

"Sure can," she says, already halfway there. Jade and I have everything else ready besides this cake I decided to stress-bake, so she tops off her wine glass.

"No mention of any of this tonight," I say to her. She mimes zipping up her lips.

———

IN NO TIME, the house is full of Velocity wives and girlfriends, also known as WAGs. Most of them are way overdressed for watching a hockey game at home, sporting tiny dresses under their winter coats. A couple even pull heels out of their purses once they get in the door.

I have learned a lot of party-hosting tricks over the last couple of years from Jade. The finger-foods are a hit, a small selection of simple refreshments are keeping everyone happy, and the party games during intermissions keep things lively when the team isn't on the ice.

We even set up a cute little selfie corner with a ring light for the women who are building their social media platforms. I thought it was silly, but Jade was adamant about it being important. I guess I wouldn't know since I don't really care about social media or being an influencer.

Brenna catches me between the second and third periods as I'm coming out of the bathroom. She's one of the few WAGs in attendance that isn't dressed to the nines. She's sporting a red Velocity hoodie with black jeans. "Hey, Carly wanted me to ask if you and Patrick are for sure coming to the wedding in two weeks. They're finalizing seating arrangements tonight."

"Wait, it's two weeks away?" I ask, brow furrowed. "I thought it was in three."

"No, it's two weeks from this Saturday."

"Shit," I say, walking into the kitchen and grabbing my phone off the top of the microwave to check our shared calendar. "I think he's got a Make-A-Wish thing going that day." Sure enough, Patrick is booked to go to Legoland Discovery Center with a kid that day.

"Do you know when he'll be back?" she asks.

I shake my head. "Knowing Pat, it'll be an all-day thing. He doesn't take them lightly. One of these days, he'll probably bring a kid home for a sleepover." I joke, but truthfully, I love my brother's big heart and that he takes his responsibilities as captain and as a sports "celebrity" seriously.

"Maybe Jade or your mom could come instead?" Brenna suggests. "Carly is being crazy about there being an even number of people. You know how she is."

"Two weeks from Saturday?" Jade asks as she walks up to us. "No can do for either of us. We're both vendors at the same bridal show in Mankato. We were just talking about it." She shrugs as she reaches in front of Brenna for the bruschetta. "Sorry, Morgs."

I push my bangs back out of my face. "Well, crap." Brenna looks worried, and I feel bad for getting the date of her best friend's wedding completely wrong. "It's all right, I'll figure something out. Tell Carly to put me down with a plus-one. I'll ask around and find someone to come with me."

In the other room, the ladies start screaming at the TV. I look over the top of someone's head and see Nils careening toward the opposing team's goalie on a breakaway. As quick as lightning, he winds up to hit the puck hard, but at the last second lets up, faking the goalie out with a softer, lower shot. With the goalie caught off-guard and off-balance, the puck glides gracefully between his legs and into the net.

Everyone in the room goes wild, cheering and high fiving each other in celebration. The Velocity are up four-to-three with only two minutes left. Their current primary goalie, Landon Jacobi, has been strong so far this season, but to pull off a win tonight would be huge.

As expected, the Winter pull their goalie from the net, giving them an extra skater to try to get past the Velocity. The puck drops for the last two minutes of the game, and all conversation ceases. We're all standing around the TV in nervous anticipation of what will happen next.

Mom sneaks quietly over to me and takes my hand in hers as we watch. Silently, we send our good vibes to the guys, willing them to hang in there and win the game.

In the last few seconds, one of the players on the Winter rifles a shot from the blue line toward the goal. It hits a stick, changing the trajectory upwards, hitting a Velocity player in the face right under his visor at a hundred miles per hour. The player collapses to the ice as the horn goes off, announcing the end of the game, but it barely registers to me. The Velocity won the game, but someone is seriously hurt.

I feel the blood drain from my face as I see my brother screaming and waving wildly for the team trainers to get on the ice.

"Is that Horvath?" one of the ladies asks out loud to the rest of us. There is so much shuffling going on in front of the net that the announcers haven't figured out who is hurt, but I knew the moment he was hit.

"It is," I say. "That's Matus."

A couple of our guys are fighting some of the Winter players as Patrick and Ryan kneel next to Matus, trying to make sure he's okay. The trainers dash as quickly across the ice as they can in their street shoes. The officials can't decide if they should be helping Matus or breaking up the fighting. The TV announcers are dumbfounded and scrambling, and they finally end up cutting away to a commercial. It's chaos.

I look down and see that my mom is gripping my hand so hard that her fingertips are white, but I don't even feel her squeeze.

Normally, we all would be celebrating a big Velocity win, but seeing one of our guys drop like that is terrifying. I've seen that kind of collapse only a handful of times before, and sadly it can be career-ending. A one-timer is one of the hardest shots someone can take in hockey, and that's what hit Matus. So, instead of celebrating, we're all silent, staring at the TV and hoping he's okay.

10

NILS

Watching a teammate fall to the ice, helpless, shook me. Seeing the sheer panic on our captain's face as he screams for the trainers has me rattled. I can't even focus on the fact that we won the game because my friend is lying face-down in a pool of his own blood.

The on-ice fighting quickly stopped once everyone realized Matus wasn't getting up. All of us on the bench are standing in silence, watching as the trainers tend to him. Even the crowd is eerily quiet – or maybe they're not, but rather everything has been reduced to a dull roar inside my head.

Distantly, I feel Coach's hand on my shoulder, urging me back to the dressing room. I turn away from the light and head into the dark tunnel.

"My line tonight with Huff and Flynn was great; those guys are both good at reading the puck and making solid plays," I say into the microphone. "When Flynn poked the puck out of there, I hit full steam ahead and got it in the five hole."

"Do you know how Horvath is doing?" one of the reporters asks.

"No, we haven't heard anything yet." I blink against the bright lights from the cameras. "He's a tough guy, and I'm sure he'll be back out there again soon."

"Congratulations again on the game winning goal. Nils Larsson, everybody. Back to you in the studio, John." The reporters thank me again, and our home station guy gives me a handshake as they pack up to head to the next interview.

I don't really enjoy post-game interviews, but I have to do them occasionally. Since I scored the game winning goal tonight, I knew I'd be asked to give one. It keeps the media, sponsors, and team owners happy.

I hightail it back to the locker room and find most of the team still in there, tensely waiting for news on Matus. I sit next to Ryan, who is texting Brenna.

"Anything?" I ask him.

"Not yet," he replies. "Did you see the video of it?"

I shake my head no. He pulls it up on his phone, and I watch the puck ricochet off the stick of one of the Winter players. It rockets under Matus's face shield, straight into his cheekbone. It's devastating to watch.

In this business, every moment on the ice is a risk. A player could get checked wrong and go head-first into the boards or fall under a skate blade and get their neck sliced or end up with a puck embedded into their face like Matus. Incidents like this are incredibly rare but sobering.

Patrick comes into the locker room with the rest of the team and our coaches. "Okay, guys. Matus is being flown back to Chicago right now. He's definitely concussed, and it looks like he may need some facial reconstruction surgery. More than likely, he'll be in the hospital for a few days and probably out for the rest of the season."

He glances around the room at each of us before continuing. "I know that isn't what we wanted to have happen right now, but it's the hand we've been dealt. We have to keep our heads up and keep fighting our way toward the playoffs."

I'm seriously bummed. Matus is a good friend and talented player. He's been strong on defense this season, so we'll certainly feel his absence.

But more importantly, I just hope he can fully recover from this.

After a few more post-game formalities from the coaches, we're packing the bus to head to the airport and finally fly home. I stare out the window of the bus, counting streetlights against the blackened sky. One of the doctors I saw when I was in treatment for my mental health taught me grounding techniques, and this works well for me.

Somewhere between the arena and airport, Patrick slides into the seat next to me. He lingers there for a few moments, neither of us looking at the other. Eventually, he puts a hand on my shoulder and leaves it there for several miles, where it serves as a full conversation without words – a conversation of fear, love, and solidarity.

11

NILS

Matus looks like hell.

I knew it would be gruesome, but I wasn't fully prepared for how rough he'd look. The puck shattered his left cheekbone. His eye is so bruised and swollen on that side that he can't open it. Under the bandages on his cheek is a long line of stitches and inevitably a future scar.

I had to come and see him. He's one of my closest friends on the team, and with his family trying to get here from Slovakia, I knew he'd need a friend right now. I know the stress of trying to get family to the U.S. from overseas in an emergency all too well.

"We won the game, right?" he asks, opening his good eye and looking in my direction.

"Yeah, man," I reply.

"Good," he says with a sigh of relief, closing his eye

and drifting back to sleep. It's the third time he's asked me about the outcome of the game.

The sun glimmers through the frost on the hospital room's window. I'm channel-surfing the TV suspended from the ceiling and eventually settle on one of the sports channels. I don't watch television very often, but it's better than sitting in silence.

The door opens, and in comes Patrick. I stand up to greet him and notice Morgan coming in behind him. My heart stops.

"How's he doing?" Patrick asks.

"He doesn't remember much about last night," I tell him. We all look over at Matus, his bruised face in stark contrast to the sterile hospital environment. "He's asked me three times if we won."

Patrick exhales next to me. His worry is palpable.

"If you don't mind, I'd like to take a walk and stretch my legs." I grab my jacket off the back of the chair. I've already been here for several hours, and I was starting to feel a little restless, but I didn't want to leave Matus by himself.

I go to move past them to the door, but Morgan says, "I'll go too. Be back soon, Pat."

I start walking down the hall toward the elevators, jacket slung over my shoulder.

"Nils, can we talk?"

I stop and turn around, finally looking at Morgan

for the first time. Her cheeks are lightly flushed from the cold air outside, and her black hair is filled with static from her jacket. I can't read her expression, but I can feel that she's nervous, as am I.

"Sure," I say as calmly as I can muster.

We head to the elevator, and she hits a button before I can even get to it. We're both silent as we descend two floors. I follow her out into the hall, where she beelines for a door labeled Chapel. She cracks it open and peeks inside.

"It's empty. Come on," she says, holding the door open for me. The chapel room is dimly lit, with a giant, metal cross hanging from the far wall. It looks like a miniature church, with three rows of wooden pews split in half for the center aisle.

Morgan and I sit in one of the pews, slightly angled to face each other.

"Are you sure we can be in here?" I ask her.

"I figured this is better than the grieving room," she says with a half-laugh. I shrug in agreement.

"So..." I start then trail off. I don't know where this conversation is going to go, nor do I really know where I *want* it to go.

I haven't been able to stop thinking about her. After the game in Boston, I ended up going out with the team, and within ten minutes, I was leaving with not one but two puck bunnies. But somehow, even while getting my dick ridden by one and my face ridden by the other, I still couldn't get Morgan off of my mind.

I'm not the only one who got laid that night. Matus ended up winning the bet against Landon. He shamelessly sent a photo to the group chat later that night of the chick with the huge boobs lying in his hotel room bed. He's got more game than anyone I know.

"So..." Morgan echoes. She looks up at me from under her long, dark eyelashes, and I think it may be the undoing of me. Infinitesimally, we move closer to each other.

"What are we doing?" I ask.

"I have no fucking clue." Her voice is barely above a whisper. "I can't stop thinking about the other day. Being on the bike with you made me feel so alive. And then everything afterwards..." A soft smile graces her lips. "I feel something between us. So when I saw an opportunity to be alone with you again, I took it. Even if it meant spilling my guts in a hospital chapel. I can't stop thinking about you, Nils."

My heart is racing in my chest, pounding into my ears, as I see nothing but this beautiful woman sharing her heart with me, despite the risks. "I can't stop thinking about you, either."

"What exactly were you thinking about?" She asks, and my dick jumps at her flirtatious tone.

"Fuck, Morgan, I want to kiss you so badly, but I'm trying to be respectful because of who you are."

"I'm Morgan," she growls. "Just Morgan. If you want to kiss me so badly, then stop talking about it and just do it."

I close the distance between us and our lips meet. Softly at first, they touch over and over, like a gentle breeze kissing the tops of trees. But quickly, the breeze escalates into a gale as our tongues intertwine.

She runs a hand along my jawline, her long, pointed nails scratching their way through my beard, sending a shiver of erotic pleasure straight down my body.

Lips still locked, I lean into her, and she slides back, propping herself against the armrest of the pew. The seat of the pew is too narrow for her body and both of my legs, so I have to plant one foot on the floor and my other knee next to her hip. It's awkward and a little uncomfortable, but it's worth it when I grind myself against her and she makes the sexiest sounds of enjoyment and need.

I hold myself up with one hand gripping the pew's armrest and slide the other hand up her maroon sweater. It's been obvious since the first time I saw her that she's well-endowed, but her breasts feel completely divine, especially when I realize she has her nipples pierced. Plus, the reaction I'm getting out of her only serves to egg me on.

We're connected at the mouth, chest, and hip, moving rhythmically against each other. I hear her breathing change, and I thrust against her a little harder, coaxing her. After only a moment, a breath catches in her throat, and I watch as she completely falls apart beneath me. It's the most sensual and beautiful thing to bring her over the brink, her face flushed and body trembling through the waves.

As her breathing finally slows, I pull my hand out of her shirt and sit back off of her. She looks at me first in post-orgasm bliss and then in terror.

"Oh my god. That is so embarrassing. I... I don't..."

"That was amazing," I tell her honestly. My dick is screaming at me in agreement and frustration.

She glances toward the door. "We should probably get out of here," she says. I stand, and after doing a little adjusting, grab my coat from the opposite end of the pew. I slide it on while she fixes her hair, and we head out into the hallway together.

"Do you think Patrick would mind if I ran home, had a shower and got something to eat, and then come back?" I ask her.

"I'm sure he'll be fine," she says quickly. "Listen...

I..." It's rare to see Morgan lost for words, but she works up her resolve and hits me with, "How soon can we do that again?"

"Um... but what about—"

"No. We are not talking about my brother. He can stay here with Matus, and he doesn't need to know what I'm doing. Answer the question."

I scratch my head, bemused and excited. "Today, my place, four pm." I want to say *right this fucking second*, but that seems a bit desperate.

She bites her bottom lip before her eyes meet mine. They're dark and filled with lust. I want her even more than I did two minutes ago.

"Okay. I'll see you at four." Then, she turns and heads for the elevators.

12

MORGAN

"I had zero intention of hooking up with Nils. I only wanted to talk, to tell him that I don't date hockey players, and the next thing I knew, I was telling him to shut up and kiss me, and he was getting me off on a fucking church pew."

And now, I'm driving to his place to hook up with him again. I have lost my fucking mind.

"Not gonna lie – that's pretty hot," Jade says, her voice coming through my car's speakers. She flew back to Minneapolis early this morning, along with my mom. "So, are you going to go through with this?"

It's been so long since another person has touched me. I had a healthy sex life late in high school and into college, and I tried to carry that into Chicago, but my cock-blocking older brother has scared off every guy that has ever even looked in my direction. Self-pleasure can only do so much for a girl, and after almost three years, I am starting to go a little insane.

Something about Nils is different. I have had good – and even what I'd consider to be great – sex in the past, but I've never been so drawn to someone the way I am to him.

Also, no guy has ever been able to get me off just through dry humping. I'm not sure if that's a check mark for him or a demerit for me.

"I'm not sure yet," I say. "I feel like I can trust him, but... he's still a hockey player. He's still on Patrick's team." I park across the street from his place and check myself one more time using my phone's camera as a mirror.

"What do you have to lose?" Jade asks. "Your brother would be mad at you and maybe kill Nils, the end. But what if you *don't* at least go in there and see what happens?"

"You're right. I don't know why I'm being so weird about this. It's just sex. I've had sex before... It's no big deal." I shut off the car and the Bluetooth disconnects, so I bring the phone to my ear as I grab my purse.

"Go get 'em, tiger," she says. "I expect a full update later!"

Shutting the car door behind me and locking it, I laugh. "Of course. You'll be the first to know."

I hang up and stare at the building again. Ready or not, here we go.

Nils answers the door almost immediately after I ring the bell. He's wearing a dark green, tightly fitted polo shirt paired with dark jeans. The shirt matches his eyes, I notice. His hair is damp and hangs loose across his broad shoulders.

My stomach does an excited flip-flop inside me.

"Come on in," he says. As I walk into his condo, I glance back at him and see his face is a mixture of happiness and hunger.

I set my purse down on his kitchen counter, kick off my shoes, and start to unzip my coat.

"Do you want a drink?" he asks.

I shake my head no.

"Damn," he says softly as my coat drops from my shoulders, showing that I'm wearing a low-cut V-neck sweater paired with my favorite skinny jeans. He moves closer until we're mere inches apart, waves of tension and chemistry crashing between us.

He swallows, his Adam's apple dropping and rising. It's all I need to lose control.

Our lips crush into each other, and I tangle my arms around his neck. He runs his hands up and down my sides, eagerly tracing the dip of my waist and the curve of my hips with his palms.

He grabs my butt and pulls me off my feet. I wrap

my legs around him, and he carries me toward his bedroom. Our lips never even break contact until he lays me on his bed.

I shed my sweater as he pulls off his shirt. The sheer white lace bra I'm wearing leaves absolutely nothing to the imagination. When he gets his shirt off and looks at me, he groans, the hunger from before now having completely taken over his face.

As he climbs on top of me, he says, "I didn't know you had your nipples pierced until earlier today."

"Well, I'd hope you wouldn't have known until today," I say with a smirk. "Do you like it?"

"God, yeah. Such a turn-on."

He takes a breast in each hand and buries his face in-between, planting kisses all over my chest, his hot breath sending shivers down my spine. I run my hands across the rippling muscles of his back. Nils isn't as bulked as most of the guys on the team, but he's in absolutely amazing shape. Perfectly muscular for his frame.

I arch my back, pressing myself against him, enjoying the feel of his body against mine. My core aches with need as I feel him growing rock-hard between my legs.

"Less clothes." His voice is nearly a growl. Hearing him so aroused only serves to fire me up even more. Enthusiastically, I nod and start unbuttoning my jeans, but his hands stop me. "Let me do it."

He unbuttons and lowers the zipper on my jeans then gently grabs the waistband to pull them down. I raise my hips to help him get them off, his hands blazing a delicate trail down my legs.

Hastily, he unzips his own jeans and throws them onto the floor. Then, he repositions himself so I can feel every inch of his hardness. The only thing between us is the thin fabric of my thong and his boxers.

Moving his hips to grind against me, he thumbs one of my nipples over my bra, then he changes his mind and takes it into his mouth, lace and all. A moan escapes me as my body reacts to his and my insides swirl with need.

His free hand slips down my stomach. When he reaches my underwear, he pushes the fabric to the side, his fingers sliding across my slick folds. I could swear that I feel every bump and groove of his fingerprints as he moves.

I'm whimpering, begging him to touch me where I need him most. He's teasing me, knowing what I want, but taking his time to give it to me.

"You're killing me," I say as I run my hand along his hip, playing with the waistband of his boxers, trying to tease him back but being too distracted to fully commit to it. After what feels like an eternity, he finally glides a finger inside me. I involuntarily contract around it, already riding so close to the edge.

"So greedy," he says with a smirk. I hold back from playfully smacking him on the arm. "I was going to take things slow, but you're ready for me already."

The next thing I know, he's pulling his boxers off as I remove my thong and kick it across the room. He grabs a condom out of his bedside drawer and rolls it on while I admire every last inch of him. My brain contains nothing but desire for him.

"Nils," I rasp.

He presses himself into me, and I gasp as my body adjusts to fit all of him. It has been too damn long, I conclude, and I'm going to make sure I never have a dry spell like that ever again.

Nils surprises me by grabbing me around the middle and pulling me up into a sitting position in the middle of the bed while he's still inside me. I wrap my legs around his torso and my arms around his head, tangling my hands into his blond locks.

Instinct takes over, and I begin to move up and down on him. It feels like fire across my skin as his hands caress my back and sides, gently urging me on, until he firmly grabs my ass with both hands and kisses my neck, whispering the magic words, "Good girl."

I'm moaning so loudly, and I don't even care. My

entire body is buzzing, alive with anticipation of the impending orgasm on the horizon.

I ride him hard, letting myself be only in this moment and nowhere else. He matches my tempo, meeting me with every thrust and touching me in all the right places. I've never had so much sexual compatibility with someone. We just fuck like the hungry animals we are.

I fight to hold back my climax for as long as possible because I don't want this to end. But it pulls me under with wave after relentless wave of pleasure. I'm fighting for air, and my entire body tingles as everything goes fuzzy. Nils thrusts a few more times before he comes completely undone.

The first time I get laid in years and it's my brother's teammate. We didn't just cross the line – we obliterated it.

13

NILS

Morgan isn't shy or quiet, but she has a wall that she hides behind. I think it's an "I'm the sister of an NHL team captain so I need to be professional" thing. It has to be tough standing in Patrick's shadow.

However, I didn't even realize she had her guard up until I saw it come down when we were fucking. I watched her come alive as our bodies met.

It was just supposed to be sex. Thrilling and forbidden, but also casual, no-strings-attached sex. But the way her body fit so perfectly against mine will never leave my memory. I want to fuck her again and again, over and over, as much as she'll have me. I want to see her come alive again and discover who she really is behind that façade.

I carefully scoot to the edge of the bed and get up.

It's four am, which means it is time for me to head to the rink for practice. It's our first home game without Matus. The team called up one of our backup guys from the AHL team, and thankfully, he's an older guy with experience playing at the NHL level. We all know him and are comfortable playing with him. This morning's practice will be important to get in sync and make sure he knows the plays we've been working on. He'll do fine, but he's no Matus, and it won't be the same.

After getting dressed and packing my gear, I gently wake up Morgan. As she gets out of bed and gathers her things, I make both of us a protein shake. She comes into the kitchen as I'm shaking the cups, one in each hand. The metal ball inside each cup clanks noisily around, mixing the ingredients.

"Can you be any louder?" she asks, playfully glaring at me from underneath her dark bangs. I toss one of the cups to her, and even though she's half-asleep, she still catches it with ease.

"Good morning to you too," I reply sarcastically then crack a smile so she knows I'm messing with her. I follow her to the foyer and throw on my leather jacket before slinging my gear bag over my shoulder.

At that moment, I realize she lives with her brother. "How are you going to explain to Patrick where you were all night?"

"He won't have a clue that I didn't come home," she says through a yawn. She rubs the sleep from her eyes, her short black hair still a disheveled mess around her face. "He goes to bed super early, and he sleeps like the dead. I could have a rave in the living room all night and he'd never even know."

"So I shouldn't tell him you stayed with me?" I joke. She glares, but a hint of a smile graces her lips.

We walk out into the bitter February morning to find the city coated in a fresh layer of snow. *Damn, no motorcycle today*, I think to myself. Morgan stands on the sidewalk, illuminated by the yellow glow of the streetlamp above her head as I lock the door behind us.

"Are you okay to drive?" I ask her. "You look exhausted."

"Yeah, I'm fine," she says with a yawn. "So, uh... I'll see you later, I guess?"

I try to read her, but the shadow of the light combined with her sleepiness makes it impossible. "For sure. Have a good day, Morgan."

Awkwardly, we turn away from each other and head our separate ways. I guess if she didn't have as great of a time as I did, then that's fine. But I hope she did because maybe she'll want to do it again. I know I do.

I reach my car and shake the thoughts of her from

my head. It's a game day, and I need to get my head in the game.

―――

THE SOUND OF MY SKATES' blades cutting fresh ice is the solace I needed. Like the throaty growl of a motorcycle engine, the sound fills my head. I let the rink take me, rushing as hard as I can from one end to the other in hopes that the burn in my legs will keep me distracted from thoughts of the beauty I had in my bed last night.

The rest of the team shows up for practice, and we get Matus's replacement into the rotation. I give my normal effort for a game-day practice and am feeling fairly confident for tonight's game.

Then, our head coach, Mike Pennington, has us all circle up.

"I know we were all hoping for better news, but I went and saw Horvath yesterday. He'll be having facial reconstruction surgery next week, after some of the swelling goes down, and the doctors believe his concussion may be a severe traumatic brain injury." Coach Mike sighs, rubbing his hand across his face. The rink is so quiet, I can hear the hum of the lights because we're all holding our collective breath. "Unfortunately, it looks like he will be out for the rest of the season.

He'll be placed on Long-Term Injured Reserve, and we'll see how things look in the fall. The staff and I are all hoping this won't be a career-ending injury for him, but, guys... realistically, it could be."

My entire body goes numb. This can't be happening to him, someone who is so integral to the organization and team, and who is also one of my closest friends.

It isn't fair. It isn't fucking fair.

Patrick is suddenly hugging me. I don't know when it happened, but I'm blinking back tears and my knees can't support my own body weight. Patrick's grip on me holds me up and keeps me present. It keeps me from spiraling into the dark place in my mind. I can't go there again, especially not right now.

I need to stay strong. For Matus.

14

MORGAN

Was it just a dream?

My phone rings, jarring me out of sleep. I roll to my side and accept Jade's video call, noting my messy hair and the bags under my eyes before her face fills the screen.

"Morgan! I've been trying to call you non-stop for the last twenty minutes! Are you okay? Are you at home?"

"Yes, I'm fine, and yes, I'm at home." I look at the clock across the room. It's already nine, and Patrick will be getting back from morning skate anytime now. "I must have been sleeping really hard."

"Must have been quite the dick to knock you out like that," she jibes.

I can't hide my grin. "God, Jade... it was incredible."

Her dark eyes go as big as silver dollars. "I need details!"

I roll over onto my stomach and prop my phone up against my pillow. Then, I rest my chin in my hands. "I walked in the house, and we didn't waste any time. Just got right down to business." I happily think back to last night and feel a mix of butterflies and fire in my belly. It's an unexpected, sweet heat. "You know, I went into it hoping for one orgasm, but I ended up having three."

She nearly chokes on her coffee. "Shut the front door! He got you off *three* times?" All I can do is grin. "Tell me *everything*."

"He was such a gentleman," I say with a smile. "He asked permission every step of the way, was down with safe sex before I had the chance to bring it up, and I swear to god, he is cut like a diamond."

"I thought you didn't like hockey players," Jade teases.

I stick my tongue out at her. "Don't remind me." It's at that moment that I hear the front door open and quickly lower the volume of my voice. "Remember, not a word about this to anyone."

She mimes zipping her lips as Patrick knocks on my bedroom door. "Come in," I say over my shoulder toward the door.

He walks in, holding the protein shake that Nils

made for me. In my stupor this morning, I must have set it down and forgotten about it. Shit. How am I going to explain this?

"This for me?" he asks. That's not at all what I expected him to ask, and I'm caught off-guard. I manage a half-nod, half-shrug. He turns and shuts my door behind him without another word.

Once I can't hear his retreating footsteps any longer, I exhale and turn back to my phone.

Jade is staring at me with an eyebrow raised. She can see in my face that I definitely didn't make a protein shake for Patrick this morning. "I can't believe he actually bought that lie. You have to be more careful or you're gonna get busted."

"I know, I know. I don't even know if anything will happen between Nils and I again, so it probably doesn't matter anyway."

"You're gonna fuck him again, I know it," Jade says with a grin.

I try to wrinkle my nose but end up grinning right back at her. "Yeah, you're probably right."

My phone dings with an incoming text from Brenna, and as I read it, my stomach instantly drops.

"Jade, I'm gonna have to call you back."

I hop out of bed and into the hallway. The door to Patrick's bedroom is shut, and I can faintly make out the sound of his shower running. I rap on his door but don't hear him respond, so I take my chances and barge in.

His ensuite bathroom door is open, but he isn't in there. Rather, he's still fully dressed in his workout clothes and sitting on the edge of his bed, his elbows on his knees and his head in his hands.

I was too caught off guard by him holding the protein shake from Nils to notice the sadness in eyes when he first came home, but it's all I see when he lifts his head to look at me. I've seen my brother cry a lot over the years, from broken bones at hockey games to broken hearts at school to a broken soul after Dad died. He's cried over a handful of brutal losses and even a couple miraculous wins in recent years too. But this is the first time that one of the guys on the team has been dealt such a shit hand since Pat took the captaincy, and I can see everything he's feeling written all over his face.

Matus is more than just a teammate to Patrick. He's a friend, a confidant, someone who is immensely loyal and supportive and so good to everyone around him. He is incredibly talented and is supposed to have a long career still ahead of him. This is about more than a game or a season or even a career. This is Patrick being devastated for Matus as a person with a potentially quality-of-life altering injury, and I'm finding myself being devastated for the both of them.

My body moves automatically to cross the space between us. I sit next to him and hold him in my arms as he cries. I cry with him. And when the tears finally subside, I continue to sit with him and allow us to exist together in the way people only can when they know each other as well as we do, with a bond that can only be formed through extreme circumstances and suffering.

15

NILS

From my place in the locker room, I can hear the arena quickly filling with the pre-game rumbles of fans and music.

I wanted to take my motorcycle out after the Matus bombshell this morning, but it snowed even more during practice, so I had to resort to running five miles on the treadmill for a little mental relief. Then, I showed up to the arena early and skated for as long as possible before the Zamboni guy kicked me off to prep the ice for the game.

At the locker next to me – Matus's locker – the call-up, a guy named Stephen Lafayette that everyone just calls Clanger because he "clangs" a lot of pucks off the goalpost, nervously turns his gloves over in his hands. He's an older guy in the hockey world and has been through several teams in the league but just hasn't managed to keep a spot at the NHL level. It's a tough league, and as he ages, the rest of the roster will continue to get younger and faster than him until he eventually fades into retirement.

I understand, in a way, the pressure he's under right now. I played in the AHL for a couple years before I eventually found a permanent spot on the Velocity's roster, so while I can't relate completely, I know that Clanger is trying to fit seamlessly into shoes that are admittedly quite big and simultaneously trying to prove that he deserves to stay up here and not be passed back down to the AHL when Matus comes back.

That is, *if* Matus comes back.

My head isn't in the game. They wipe the floor with us in a disgusting five-to-two loss. Of course, all five goals can't be blamed on me, but I know I wasn't focused, and it showed on the ice. However, I don't think Coach will end up reaming me out for it. Most of the team played pretty awful.

For what it's worth, Clanger actually had a decent game, scoring one of our goals of the evening. Under different circumstances, I'd be happy for him. But I wish it were Matus playing, so I just can't muster any praise for him without it feeling inauthentic.

We have an optional practice tomorrow then practice and another home game the next day. I hope I can get myself out of this funk before then.

I check my phone after a post-game shower at the arena and see a text from Morgan.

> Hey, I just wanted to check and see if you're okay.

She had to work at the pub tonight and more than likely watched our abysmal performance on TV.

> I'm hanging in there.
>
> Can I see you tomorrow?

She immediately responds.

> I work in the morning, but I can come over after I get out. Is that okay?

I shoot her back an affirmative and tuck my phone into my pocket as I head out the basement doors into the underground parking structure that is reserved for the players, team staff, and league staff.

I'm almost to my car when I see Ryan and Patrick

standing by Ryan's car. They both look as dejected as I feel. I walk over to them.

"I've seen guys take some bad hits and some nasty shots before, but it really takes just one wrong angle to end your entire career," Ryan says.

"Don't say that," I say as I approach, my voice low. "We don't know that for sure yet."

"May as well be the end of his career," Ryan replies. "It's the end of our playoff hopes, that's for sure."

"Flynn," Patrick growls. "Just stop. Okay? We have to stay positive for him and for ourselves."

Ryan sighs next to me, his shoulders visibly sagging. "I'm trying, man. I really am."

Patrick turns to stare across the parking lot, his brows furrowed. After a moment, without turning toward us, he says, "Don't you guys remember when Detroit had a player get in an accident right after they won the Cup back in the nineties? That guy was permanently injured and never played again. You know what that team did? Came back the next season and won the championship for him. They had him on the ice, wheelchair and all, and helped him lift the Cup."

Ryan and I are quiet, knowing Patrick isn't done yet. When he finally turns to look at us, his eyes are full of fire. "Don't you see? We are that team now. We have to win the Cup – for Matus."

I AM the first person at the hospital's front desk to check in when visiting hours start at eight the next morning. Matus is asleep when I quietly let myself into his room, setting down my travel mug of hot tea and taking up residence on the couch next to his bed.

I watch the sun rise across the snowy cityscape, its rays glittering across the snowflakes and glass structures. The gentle beeps and whirring of machines next to Matus's bed creates a soft soundtrack that fills me with melancholy. I hate the idea of him being in here alone, even when he's just sleeping, so I've decided to spend as much time here with him as I can.

Fiddling on my phone gets old after a bit, but I can't let myself feel negatively about being bored when I've chosen to be here of my own free will. I am healthy and not the person who is injured.

I decide to meditate to work through my emotions, but only a minute later, Matus stirs. I open my eye a crack and meet his gaze.

"What're you doing here?" he asks, his voice thick with sleep – or maybe this is how he sounds now, with a brain injury and barely being able to move his mouth. He still looks like absolute hell, the bruising continuing to darken and spread across his face. Abandoning my meditation, I untuck my legs from under me and stand, moving closer to him.

"I wanted to check on you," I reply as I kneel next to him. "How're you feeling?"

"Like I took a fuckin' puck to the face. How else?" He tries to smile but can't quite move enough of his face to do so convincingly, although hearing the humor in his voice lifts my spirits a bit.

"You look like hell," I say. "How're you going to get any girls now with that ugly mug?"

"You're one to talk," he retorts, a glint in his eye. "Check a mirror, fucker."

I can't help but grin, and I damn near tell him about that wild and passionate night with Morgan. Thankfully, my brain catches up with my mouth and shuts it down.

Matus is my friend who is laid up in a hospital bed, barely able to move or talk. He may not even remember this conversation. But I'm not quite ready to kiss and tell. Even if it would give me incredible cred with the rest of the team.

"You know, the team is talking about doing a fundraiser for you, to help with your medical bills and all that."

"If they paid me more, they wouldn't need to fundraise for me," he replies with a chuckle, then he winces. "Fuck, everything hurts."

I notice his hand fumbling around in the bed, looking for something. "What do you need?"

"They gave me a pain button. Push it and get more drugs." He finds the off-white remote somewhere under the blankets and pushes one of the buttons on it. The machine it's attached to starts beeping, signaling that it is dosing medication into the IV in Matus's forearm.

"Damn, get me one of those," I joke.

Just then, a nurse comes in, smiling from ear to ear. "Matus, I'm glad you're awake. Your family just called. They made it through customs and will be here in just a bit."

"Thanks, Lacey," he replies, and I think he tries to wink at her with his one eye that isn't swollen shut. She closes the door behind her, and I turn back to him.

"Do you know all of the nurses' names?"

"Of course I do."

I smirk. He might be badly injured, but thankfully, he's still Matus.

16

MORGAN

Two Bits is fairly quiet this morning. I'm thankful for the calm because I worked last night and dealing with chaos at open always sucks. I don't like doing close-opens, but one of the servers had a family emergency, so I offered to cover her shift. Unfortunately, Danielle is working the bar this morning, and she's extra bitchy.

I drop off a heaping plate of breakfast nachos at one of the tables and head up to the bar to grab a drink of my water. I can feel Danielle's contemptuous gaze tracking me as she continues to dry the same glass she's been working on for a while now. Avoiding her is tough when it's only her, me, and one other server working this morning.

The front door chimes to announce someone coming in, and my heart skips a beat when I see the familiar stance of Nils. He looks absolutely ravishing in a dark grey, wool peacoat and black jeans, his long locks disheveled from the wind.

But it's his smile that pulls me in.

Danielle is quickly forgotten as I cross the pub to greet him. "Hey," I say with a smile. "You're here earlier than I expected."

He shrugs off the peacoat as we walk together toward the bar, revealing a white, cable-knit sweater underneath. "Matus's family just arrived, and I wanted to give them some time alone with him." He hangs his coat on the back of the chair and takes a seat at the end of the bar.

"I'm so glad they made it." I sigh with relief as I stand next to him. "I'm sure getting flights on such short notice was a nightmare."

"Hi, Nils," comes Danielle's sing-song voice, sickeningly sugary-sweet. "What'll it be?"

"Hi, Danielle," he says politely. "Just a water for now."

She quickly scoops ice into the glass she had been drying for half the morning and then pours water into it, setting it in front of Nils. "Here you go," she says, her voice a mixture of silk and velvet. "Let me know if you need anything else, okay?" She smiles at him before turning to me with a frown. "Shouldn't you check on table twenty-three, Morgan? Their drinks have been empty for a while."

"Thanks, Danielle," I say through gritted teeth. I cross the pub to table twenty-three, whose drinks aren't actually empty, and check on them. I check with my other three tables then glance over at the bar.

Danielle has her elbows on the edge of the bar right in front of Nils, her chin resting in her hands, deep in conversation with him. I notice she's wearing a particularly low-cut top today, giving him quite the show. I try not to let my anger bubble up under my skin. First, she flirts with my brother constantly, and now with the guy I like?

Not that she knows I like him. Does she? Does *he*? Fuck.

I quickly take the drink orders for a couple that just sat down and stomp over to the computer to put them into the system. Thank God they both ordered mimosas so Danielle has to actually do something rather than shove her tits in Nils's face. I stare at her from the computer station until she finally notices she has an order in and peels herself away from her position in front of him.

This shift can't go by fast enough, I think to myself.

Steve pops his head out of the kitchen door, and I see his face light up when he spots Nils. As I approach the bar, I see Danielle roll her eyes with her back to Steve as he comes out to shake Nils's hand.

"How're things? How's Horvath?" Steve asks him.

"He was in good spirits this morning," Nils says. "He made a couple jokes when I was there."

"That's so good to hear." Steve wipes the sweat from his brow with the edge of his apron. Danielle places the two mimosas in front of me and turns her attention to the guys.

"What bad luck, to take a shot like that," Steve continues. He clicks his tongue, and I see Danielle visibly flinch at the sound. "Anyway, good to see you, man. Let me know if there's anything I can do for Matus, yeah?" He starts to head back into the kitchen.

Nils glances at me. I can't read the expression on his face. "Actually, there might be."

Steve turns back around, an eyebrow raised.

"I think the Velocity organization wants to do a fundraiser for Matus," says Nils. "Any chance it could be hosted here?"

"Say no more, my boy! Of course it can be hosted here!" Steve claps his hands together, genuinely giddy. "Morgan, you'll let me know dates and times and such, yeah?"

I nod enthusiastically, still a bit surprised but there's excitement building. "Yeah, definitely. I'll get in touch with the marketing department to get it hashed out and let you know what they're wanting." Between Jade's party-planning skills and my connections with both Two Bits and the team, I'm confident we could throw a great fundraiser for Matus.

"Is that really such a good idea, Steve?" asks Danielle drily. "I mean, the Velocity could use any venue in the city. Wouldn't it feel like they're taking advantage of us just because Morgan works here? They'd probably expect a big discount to use the pub, and that feels wrong to me."

If I could kill someone with just a glare, Danielle would be dead. She doesn't give two shits about the pub on any normal day. Of course, anything that involves me is bad in her little world.

"Not at all," Steve says pleasantly, oblivious to Danielle's attempt at undermining and sabotaging my chance to help be part of something awesome. God bless his ignorance. "They're like family. Matus is a great kid, and if the team wants to use our place, I'm fine with it. Besides, it could be good for business too."

Scorned, Danielle turns around and fiddles with the liquor bottles as Steve heads back into the kitchen and I take mimosas to my table. The rest of the morning, my mind is consumed equally by thoughts of the fundraiser and that handsome hockey player sitting at the bar waiting for my shift to end.

17

MORGAN

Once my shift is finally done, Nils and I grab lunch at the deli down the block from Two Bits before getting into our separate cars and both heading to his place. I park across the street from his condo, and he meets me at the front door.

"Fancy seeing you here," he says as he opens the door for me, his mouth quirking upwards into a smile. I feel my body hum in tune with the electricity passing between us.

"You're in an awfully good mood today," I say to him as I hang my coat on the hook by the door. "I think you said more words to Steve today than every other conversation you've had with him combined."

He puts his hands on my hips, and my breath catches in my throat at the contact. "Probably," he muses with a smile. "Seeing Matus today and hearing him joke around put me in a good place." He looks into my eyes, searching back and forth between them. "Plus, I get to see you too. How could I not be happy?"

I wrap my arms around his waist and pull us closer. I bury my face into his chest, the sweater tickling my cheek as I run my hands up and along his back. His hands move to my lower back and tighten the hug as he rests his cheek on top of my shoulder.

Nils's struggle with depression isn't well known in the league. But being Patrick's sister means I occasionally get to know things others don't – or I accidentally find out things I'm not supposed to know.

It was purely by chance that I walked into the house as Pat got the call from Coach that Nils was in a treatment facility two years ago. Of course, Pat told me I couldn't tell anyone, and I didn't, not even Jade.

He missed a few games with an "undisclosed injury," came back, and life went on. He doesn't talk about it, and to my understanding, things have been better.

I know Patrick checks in with Nils often and worries about him a lot. My brother carries a lot more emotional weight than most people realize, and he truly cares about his teammates. It's reassuring that Nils has Patrick to rely on if things get hard again.

Seeing Nils so happy today and knowing I had a hand in it fills my chest with warmth.

I feel myself falling for him, hard and fast.

And I don't even care.

I lean harder into him, pressing my hips against his and arching my back. He immediately responds by finding my neck with his lips. He starts walking us, still connected, to the bedroom.

When I check my phone later, I see I have a text from Brenna asking if I found a plus-one for Carly's and John's wedding. I had completely forgotten about it, but I'm sure Carly hadn't let Brenna forget. They met in college and were roommates for a while.

However, Brenna and Ryan recently moved in together, which Brenna told me has been a saving grace for their strained friendship. I guess Carly has been a bit of a bridezilla. And I think it's become an "absence makes the heart grow fonder" kind of situation for them.

Back to the issue at hand... I need a date to a wedding.

Nils is sitting in the bed next to me, his back against the headboard, reading a book in Swedish. He looks so relaxed and peaceful, even with his blond hair an absolute mess atop his head.

He's the obvious choice to ask. Patrick is busy, Jade is busy, Brenna is in the wedding, and I don't know or like any of the rest of the team's WAGs enough. Harsh, but true. Most of them are catty, wannabe social media influencers, and that just isn't me.

But I can't just turn up at a wedding with Nils as my date. Can I? Although, it wouldn't be a date. Two people can attend an event and not have it be a date. Right?

Screw it, here goes nothing.

"Hey," I say.

"Yeah?" He looks up from his book.

"I'm supposed to attend this wedding next Saturday for Brenna's friend that I kind of know, and I have to bring a plus-one, but Patrick has a Make-A-Wish event, and Jade has a wedding thing, and Brenna will already be there, and my mom–"

"Yes, I'll go with you." He cuts me off, smirking. I must look dumbfounded. "What's that look for?"

"I didn't expect you to want to go to a wedding for people you don't even know," I say.

He sticks a bookmark in his book and closes it. "Why wouldn't I? I don't have anything planned that day."

"Well, you don't know all of the details yet," I

reply. "Ryan and Brenna will both be there. Won't they ask questions about why we're there together?"

"I would say that you needed a plus-one and I was available," he says gently. I fiddle with my phone, turning it over and over in my hands. "You're nervous of what Patrick will think."

"Of course I am," I say. "Don't you remember what he did to Daniels when he grabbed my ass a couple of years ago?"

I hesitate to call it assault, even though pretty much anyone else but me would. Corey Daniels, a longtime goalie for the Velocity and several years my senior, pulled that shit at a fundraiser and several people saw it. Patrick proceeded to beat the absolute shit out of him in front of the team, owners, media... everyone. It was a PR nightmare for all of us. Patrick had to issue a public apology to the event coordinators and to Corey.

"It will be okay," he says. "We are just two friends attending an event together. If it would make you feel better, I can mention to Patrick that I will be your plus-one so he isn't surprised."

"Absolutely not. Are you crazy?"

Nils grins at me. "Maybe."

I sigh. "He will handle it better if it comes from me. He should be fine after I reassure him a hundred times that you're just going to fill the gap in Carly's seating chart."

He reaches out to brush a hand along my cheek, a look in his eyes I can't quite place, before returning his attention to the book he was reading.

I feel relieved, and yet, part of me wishes he *was* going as my date.

I have to remind myself once again that even if we wanted to be an actual couple, there's no way Patrick would let that slide.

18

NILS

A few days and an away game later, Morgan is back at my house slinging cocktail creations.

"I worked on a few ideas while you were gone," she says over her shoulder as she pours vodka into a shot glass. "I think I have a couple of good ones, but I really want to know what you think."

I lean against the counter and watch as she pours her heart into the drink she's crafting. I swear she's glowing. This is the confident, happy, and free girl who rode on the back of my motorcycle, and I could watch her all night. "Good thing I'm thirsty."

Her head snaps over to look at me, her black hair swinging around the sides of her face. She raises an eyebrow at me, and I can see she's struggling to hold back a smile.

I thought about her a lot on our short road trip. I'm enjoying getting to know her, and the extra physical benefits have been pretty damn great too. I can't complain. I didn't even hook up with anyone while I was gone – a rarity for me. I just didn't feel the need to.

Although there isn't anything official between us, I like what I have with Morgan. I turned down several women without so much as a second thought. They were pissed, but I didn't care. All I could think about was getting back to Chicago so I could see her.

She pours various liquids into cups as I let my eyes rake over her body. She's wearing a dark red tank top with a little black lace coverup and black jeans. And she's not wearing a bra. I can make out the outline of her piercings through the tank top. I wanted to jump her the minute she arrived, but she was excited about her cocktails, so I'm trying to restrain myself.

Trying, being the key word.

"Okay, here's the first one." She slides a glass over to me, breaking me out of my thoughts.

Twenty minutes later, the third drink is a hit. "This one is the best yet," I say, holding it up to eye level. "I think you're on to something here."

"Really?" Morgan's eyes light up across the kitchen island.

"Really," I affirm. "It's smoky and spicy and sweet

and... wow." I take another drink from the glass, savoring the aromas and flavors. "What is it?"

"It's a Paloma, but I infused the syrup with jalapeños and—"

"Say no more. It's perfect." I cut her off. Her smile is a mile wide. "If Steve doesn't like this better than whatever Danielle makes, then he's crazy."

"What a relief," she says happily. She comes around the kitchen island to me and wraps her arms around my waist, burying her face into my chest. "Thank you so much for being my guinea pig. I seriously appreciate it."

I hug her back. "You're so welcome. But I still don't get why they chose that animal out of all of them."

"Don't question weird English phrases," she says with a laugh. "You know this language makes little sense."

As we let go, our eyes meet. A spark passes between us. She bites her lip, and I'm aware of every inch of her body that is touching mine. I know she's waiting for me to make the first move.

The side of her face in one hand, I pull her mouth to mine in a hot kiss. She tastes like a mixture of all the drink concoctions we tried tonight. Her hip in my other hand, I pull her body against me. Her hands immediately slip under my shirt and pass over my abs and chest.

My reaction is primal. I pull my shirt over my head and toss it. It doesn't even hit the floor before I'm pulling her tank top over her head, her breasts bouncing as they pop free of their fabric prison. The lace coverup falls to the floor, tangled in the tank top.

I pull away from her in a moment of clarity. I start to reach into my wallet, but she stops me.

"We don't have to use a condom if you don't want to," she says. "I've been on birth control for years for my periods."

"Are you sure?" I ask her. "I was clean at my last STI screening at the beginning of the season, and I've used protection every time since then, but if you want to wait for me to get tested again—"

Her lips capture mine, cutting me off as her hands work at the button on my jeans. She tugs them down my thighs, and her jeans and underwear quickly follow. My hands hold her body against mine, creating a friction that is quickly reaching dangerous voltage.

"I want you, all of you, with nothing separating us," she says, her voice filled with lust.

I feel my cock somehow get even harder. "I want that too."

I grab her shoulders and spin her around so she's

facing away from me then nudge her to the edge of the kitchen island. I square up directly behind her and gently press between her shoulder blades so she bends over the counter.

Guiding my dick to her, I push in slowly but with purpose, filling her. It feels absolutely unreal. Her moans fill the room. We're both so damn loud when we fuck. Thank God I don't have a roommate.

My hands make their way to the curve in her hips, the spot where they meet her waist, and I hold her there as I pull back and push in again. I watch the way her ass shakes as I slam into her.

"Pull my hair," she says breathily. I leave one hand on her hip, and I entangle my fingers in her hair with the other.

"Tell me if it's too much," I say. She nods.

We move in rhythm, fucking like goddamn animals on my kitchen island. She's feral; her moaning borders on screams as I pound into her from behind. It's fast and hot, and before I know it, she begins to come undone under me, sending me into a frenzy. I climax only a few thrusts later, crying out with her, savoring every pulse of our connected bodies.

Once everything starts to come back into focus and my head clears from the fog of euphoria, I carefully pull out of her. I step out of my jeans and boxers bunched up at my feet. I walk into the bedroom and quickly return with a couple towels.

She hasn't moved yet. She's still bent over the island, resting across the granite, the insides of her thighs dripping wet and gloriously spread for me.

I could totally go for another round.

19

MORGAN

"Well, this one is... better than the last one, at least," Carly says with a sigh. Brenna just stares at herself in the mirror, a look of contemplation on her face before finally deflating.

"I think I have tried on fifty dresses at this point," Brenna whines.

This one isn't bad. But it is getting hard to keep them all straight after seeing so many this morning. I don't even remember which ones I liked anymore.

"You know Ryan will be drooling over you no matter which dress you wear," I offer.

"I know," she groans. "But..."

"You only get married once... hopefully. And you don't want to get eaten alive by the gossip sites," I repeat back the concerns she mentioned earlier today. They're valid concerns, but considering she's only been engaged for a few weeks, and they haven't even set an official, solid wedding date yet, I think she's overthinking everything.

Brenna struggles a lot with her self-image. She's pretty in the girl-next-door kind of way, which has to be difficult when your best friend is gorgeous in the social-media-influencer kind of way.

With Carly's wedding being only two weeks away, and Brenna being her maid of honor, they've been spending a lot more time together again. And I can see Brenna's self-confidence waning. Old habits die hard, apparently, but I refuse to let her lose herself again.

"Try getting into Ryan's head really quick," I say. She starts to make a face, but I cut her off. "Just humor me, Bren. Think about you and Ryan. It drives him wild when you wear…?"

She stares at the mirror thoughtfully, chewing her nail. "He seems to like the simple things most."

"Okay, we're getting somewhere."

A slow smile spreads across her face. "I think I've seen the perfect dress." She spins around to the bridal shop consultant, who looks positively annoyed with us. "I saw it over here on the mannequin."

Carly and I sit in awkward silence after Brenna and the consultant disappear to find the dress. She fiddles with her freshly filled acrylic set, and I cycle through the social media apps on my phone.

I don't know Carly all that well; we were forced together and bonded, in a way, when Brenna was going through some shit a few months ago.

Although we are connected through Brenna, I wouldn't call Carly and I "friends." She seems a little too high maintenance for me. She'd probably get along well with some of the hockey girlfriends. They could probably give each other selfie tips or share the latest trending hashtags...

"Brenna mentioned you all might drop by the pub tonight on your bachelorette route," I say to Carly.

She glances at me over her nails. "Yeah, we might come through there."

"Cool," I say. "I'll be working tonight. Sorry I wasn't able to get the night off."

She shrugs dismissively and the conversation dies. Oh well, I guess. Can't say I didn't try to connect with her. It's not my fault she's as icy as Zimmerman Arena, where the team plays. And I didn't really want to go anyway.

I go back to my phone and pull up my texts with Nils. I sent him a sexy photo of myself this morning, and he's been sending drooling emojis and GIFs of all the naughty things he wants to do to me the next time he sees me.

Our sexual chemistry is off the charts. And for now, we both seem to be on the same page – no strings. Not that we've had an actual conversation about it. We hang out a lot, but we definitely spend more time fucking than talking.

Not like Patrick would be okay with any of it, but what he doesn't know won't hurt him.

A smiling, reinvigorated Brenna and the bridal shop consultant reappear with the dress and disappear into the dressing room. I send another scantily clad mirror selfie to my favorite Swede and smile to myself when he instantly replies back with a string of emojis, including fire, heart eyes, and eggplants.

20

NILS

Matus stares at Patrick as best as he can. The bruising and swelling on his face has finally peaked, for now. Once it comes down a bit, they'll be ready to do plastic surgery to repair the damage, but in the meantime, his eye is a slit behind purple, swollen skin.

Patrick sits across from me, his face sullen. The dark circles under his eyes are already apparent on his downcast face, but the harsh hospital lights aren't doing him any favors.

"I can't believe I'm going to miss our first real shot at the Stanley Cup," Matus mumbles, his accent thicker than normal due to being around his family and speaking his native Slovak so much over the last few days.

They moved Matus to LTIR, or Long-Term

Injured Reserve, as of today. The team was waiting for official word from his doctors before declaring him unfit to play and eligible for LTIR. A player can miss ten games after an injury before they have to be moved off the roster to LTIR. Even though anyone could clearly tell just by looking at Matus that ten games would not be enough for recovery. Whatever the men in the suits want, I suppose.

"It's shitty," Patrick says glumly. He looks up. "You know I'd trade places with you in an instant if I could."

"Don't," Matus says sternly as he looks at his hands in his lap. "Don't, Huff. You know this team wouldn't have a goddamn chance in hell of winning without you."

Patrick sighs in resignation, knowing better than to argue with Matus, especially when we all know he's right. Sure, it'll be difficult to win without Matus in the lineup, but it won't be impossible. We truly rely on Patrick's steady, level-headed leadership and high expectations. Without Matus, we'll struggle, but we'd be doomed without Patrick.

Turning his head as much as he can to face Patrick, Matus's voice is stern and resolved. "Go kick some ass and get us into the playoffs. And then, win the whole goddamn thing. I'll be in the stands when you lift the Cup. I swear it."

———

THE WEATHER IS STARTING to tease spring as I take the bike through the congested streets near Millennium Park. Tourists are flocked around The Bean, a giant silver statue in the shape of a legume. I watch them, bemused, as I sit behind a charter bus at a red light. I hear that in Los Angeles, it is legal to ride your motorcycle in-between lanes of cars to get through traffic faster. I don't know how true that is, but I'd never dare do that here in Chicago, unless I had a death wish. Chicago drivers are something else.

Morgan is working tonight, and I'll be in Florida for an away game for the next couple of days, so I'm heading to Two Bits to hang out during her shift. I know it's not the same as alone time at my house, but I'll miss her while I'm gone, so I'll take what I can get while I'm here.

A short while later, I park the bike in the covered entryway to the kitchen door in the back alley of the pub. Perks of being an NHLer who hangs out here a lot. One time, when I mentioned parking a bike was a nightmare in the city, Steve, the owner, told me to "just pull 'er straight into the kitchen." That seemed a bit excessive, so I compromised with parking outside the door. It only gets used for deliveries in the morning anyway and has a security camera just in case someone tries to jack my bike.

The pub is decently busy tonight, but my favorite seat at the bar is still open, so I grab it. Morgan's eyes light up when she sees me, and she quickly pours me a beer.

"Hey, you," she says quickly. We exchange a smile before she hits the next drink order coming through the ticket system.

I shoot her a wink as I sip my beer and grin as she blushes. There's an elegance to the way she moves around the bar. I'm sure it comes with years of working here, learning where everything is and getting into a comfortable groove. She's in her element here. It reminds me of sharing the locker room with a seasoned vet in the league. There is just something about the easy, sure movements that comes with experience and confidence.

Also, the tight, cropped black shirt that exposes her midriff and accentuates her hips and cleavage certainly helps keep my attention too.

Steve comes in from the kitchen, surveying the busy pub. He doesn't normally work this late in the evening, so they must be short-staffed in the kitchen. He wipes his brow on the towel from his apron pocket. "Morgan, how're things out here?"

"We're surviving," she says, her voice a bit strained.

"Of course, the night the entire kitchen and half the servers call off, we are slammed. The girls have been explaining to everyone we're short in the kitchen tonight in hopes people will just drink and order easy items to help you out as much as we can. How're you doing back there?"

"I had to come get some fresh air," Steve says as he helps himself to a clean glass and begins pouring water into it.

"Steve!" I hear Danielle's shrill, scolding voice from behind me. I notice Steve wince ever so slightly. "I just put in three more orders! What are you doing out here?"

"Just getting a drink," he says to her, raising his glass for her to see. He sighs, and as he turns to head back into the kitchen, he notices me. "Nils! How are you, my friend?"

"Hey, Steve. I'm fine," I say. "Are you okay? Do you need some help?"

He looks at me, evaluating. I can see the exhaustion in his face. He isn't exactly a young man. "What the hell? You're hired. Get your ass back here."

21

MORGAN

I haven't had my ass kicked this badly by a shift in a long, long time. My feet and back hurt now, but it will be even worse tomorrow. With just Steve, me, Danielle, and the two basically brand-new servers in the pub tonight, it's been a nightmare of a Saturday night. I offered to help Steve in the kitchen when I realized how short we were, but he refused my help – only because the newbies are too new to run the bar, and Danielle said she couldn't do bar because she was wearing new jeans and didn't want to get them all sticky. Selfish bitch. I hope she accidentally spills something on them tonight.

Somehow, Nils has ended up back in the kitchen with Steve. Good thing, because as soon as he showed up, we got even busier with food orders. Yet, the tickets kept flowing and we didn't completely crash and burn.

It's late into the evening, and the pub is beginning to clear out. I haven't seen Carly, Brenna, and the rest of the crew, so I assume they decided to skip Two Bits on their bachelorette party adventures. That's probably for the best since I wouldn't have been able to talk to them in the chaos anyway.

I pop back into the kitchen to check on a food order and find Nils at the fryer. He looks dorky and adorable in his kitchen apron as he drops an order of fries into the oil.

"Hey," I yell at him over the sound of potatoes deep frying. He grins at me, his skin slick with grease and sweat. "Table twenty-seven wants no salt on those fries."

He brings one hand up to his face in a salute. "Yes, ma'am!"

I can't help but smile and laugh. "Steve, how are you two doing back here?"

"We're good!" he says cheerfully as he flips a burger patty on the grill. "Nils might be the best sous chef I've ever had. If he wasn't such a damn good hockey player, I'd hire him in a heartbeat!"

I pretend to be insulted. "There's no way he's a better sous chef than me!"

Steve lobs a tomato slice at me, which I barely manage to dodge, and it hits the ground. "Hush. No one will take your place in my heart. Now, will you run this plate to table three?"

Sticking my tongue out at him, I grab the plate and start to head for the doors. Looking back, I see Nils and Steve laughing together, and although my body is tired, my heart is happy.

———

"Go home," I tell Steve again. "Nils and I got this."

"If you're sure..." He trails off. I pull the apron from his hands and push him toward the door.

"Yes, we are sure," Nils says over my shoulder. "Get some rest."

Resigned, Steve nods. "Thank you both. We wouldn't have survived tonight without the two of you." He heads for the door but then stops suddenly. "Oh, yeah. Morgan? Can you come by tomorrow morning and make your drink? I want to give it a try."

"Of course. I'll see you tomorrow," I reply.

Steve heads out into the night, and I lock the front door behind him. Nils hits the light switch for our open sign out front to turn it off. I sent the newbies home an hour ago, and Danielle sent herself home once she decided she was done for the night, I guess.

"What a night," he says, one hand on his hip as he looks around the pub. "Well, you have fun, I'm going to nap in this booth over here." He sees my face and laughs. "Kidding, kidding!"

"You're lucky you're cute, Nils Larsson. Let's get this done. There are so many other things I'd rather be doing with you right now." I hand him a broom.

"Like what?" He tries to trap me in his arms, but I slide out of his grip.

"Do a good job and maybe you'll find out," I say with a laugh.

There's a lot of work to do in order to close up, but I'm so thankful Nils is here with me. As we work, we talk. I mean, we usually talk, but this time we *talk* – hopes, dreams, fears. The hours feel like minutes, and the work is easy with him by my side.

This feels so natural. This feels so right.

Finally, everything is finished. I don't even want to look at the clock because I am sure it will just be depressing. I sigh from my barstool and put my forehead onto the freshly washed bar top. "I am too tired to move. I will just sleep right here tonight."

He comes up behind me and wraps his arms around my waist, pressing his face into my back. "Okay," he says with a smile in his voice. Then, slowly, his hands spread out and move their way up my torso, cupping my breasts.

"How do you still have energy for that?" I ask him as he gently caresses them over my shirt.

"I always have energy for you," he replies in a low, throaty voice. "Especially when you look so sexy." I feel that familiar hum start low in my body as he slips his hands under my crop top and bra, sliding his fingers across the skin close to my nipples. I can't help my body's response to his touch as I arch my back, trying to press myself into his hands. He takes advantage by putting his lips to the side of my neck, close to my ear. "I want to fuck you on top of the bar," he whispers.

"Well, in that case..." I smirk. Quickly, I climb onto the top of the bar. I pull my shirt and bra over my head in one motion and toss them to the floor as I lean back on the smooth wooden surface. The cool veneer against my shoulder blades sends a light shiver down my spine. Nils is matching my pace, already taking his shirt off and working on his jeans as I lift my hips to shimmy my pants past my hips.

I'm left wearing nothing but my dark green thong as he climbs onto the bar top with me, completely naked, and settles in between my legs. I've learned that he likes to be able to remove my underwear himself, so I've left it on for him. He leans over me, propped on his hands and knees, blond hair falling across his emerald eyes.

We kiss and it instantly warms me against the chill of the bar surface. His lips are soft, and his stubble scratches against the skin around my mouth. I can tell he's hungry for me. An evening of hard labor has worked up an appetite that I'm happy to satisfy.

He kisses his way across my jaw and down my neck, lowering himself to my body like he's doing a pushup but making it look far easier than they ever were for me in high school gym class. I see a smile on his face before he takes my right nipple into his mouth, instantly sending a new wave of desire burning through me. He's gotten really good at sucking on them without undoing the metal barbell jewelry.

Continuing his way down my body, he kisses a slow trail from my nipples to my belly button. He pauses, sitting back on his heels, and gently runs his fingertips across the thin fabric on my hips.

"You're killing me," I growl as my hips involuntarily buck. His dick is fully hard, teasing me from a distance, just out of reach.

"Patience." By the tone of his voice, you'd think he was asking. But I know better. This is Nils in control, in a way I've never seen before.

Gently, his right hand travels across the lace. He hooks his index finger under the edge of the garment and pulls it to one side. While holding it there, he deftly runs his remaining fingers across my folds, eliciting a needy whine from somewhere within me. The sound must register with him because he finally caves to my impatience, and I feel him press two fingers into me.

His free hand grasps his dick, and he begins to move both hands in rhythm. My hips match the motion as I force him deeper into me, gyrating in a way to grind my clit against his palm.

"You are awfully greedy for someone who was tired ten minutes ago," he chides me with a grin.

"I can't help what you do to me," I breathlessly reply. I'm squirming, my body begging for more contact. He's too far away from me to touch, so I resort to running one hand through my own hair and using the other to play with the nipple he didn't suck on earlier.

I delight in looking at him in the dimmed lighting of the bar, the shadows playfully highlighting his defined muscles. His abs flex with his uneven breath. The muscles in his arm flex as his fingers move within me. And of course, watching him stroke himself while touching me only makes me even hungrier for him.

The burning within me starts to ramp up, and he senses the change. I whimper as he pulls his fingers out of me but enjoy watching him lick me off of them. He's teasing me, his eyes fixed on me as his tongue drags across his slicked fingers.

"You want me?" His hands grip my thighs.

"Yes," I half-moan, half-growl.

"Good girls ask nicely," he reminds me, squeezing my thighs tighter.

My hips involuntarily buck lightly and a raspy breath escapes me.

"Say please."

"Please, Nils. Please," I beg.

His hands slide up my thighs to my thong, where they grab the waistband. I raise my hips to allow him to slide it down. He shifts his body to the side in order to move the thong down both of my legs, which I appreciate. Him ripping all my pretty lingerie was getting expensive. He then takes his place between my legs again, using his knees to push them farther apart as he scoots into position.

My breath escapes me when he finally presses himself inside me. I'm so glad we ditched the condoms and I get to truly *feel* him. And I'm so close to the edge already, filled with desire, and now filled with him too.

I lift my legs and wrap them around his waist, allowing him to hit even deeper, and he groans with pleasure at the position shift. He fucks me intensely. It isn't nearly as feverish as we usually do, but it isn't slow either. His rhythm is steady and determined. I desperately hold on to the side of the bartop, trying to keep from sliding now that my back is slick with sweat. We're both fighting to hang on for as long as we can, but his jagged breaths in my ear push me closer to the edge.

With one hand in my hair, he tells me, "You're such a fucking good girl," and it's my undoing. The orgasm is a rocket; I instantly fracture into a million pieces beneath him, my back arching, pressing every part of me against every part of him.

He manages a few more thrusts, frantically chasing me into the abyss. With the sexiest moan I've ever heard, he reaches his climax. I clench around his shaft as he comes and revel in the feeling of him pulsating within me.

Thoroughly spent, he rests his head on my chest, his hands holding the sides of my waist and his cock still inside me. I gently play with his hair, savoring the peaceful moment.

"You're amazing, *min kära*," he whispers, and before I can ask, he translates, "My dear."

My heart squeezes in my chest.

22

NILS

I despise the treadmill. I'd rather run on a track or across a field or literally anywhere except a treadmill. However, we came back from an away game in Tampa to a fresh layer of snow and subzero temperatures, so no outdoor running for my workout today.

Patrick climbs onto the treadmill next to me, his skin covered in a glistening sheen of sweat from the bench press. We exchange a friendly nod before he turns on the machine and starts to jog.

I wonder if he has any clue that I've been fucking his sister. I honestly don't think he knows. I am well aware that anyone who even glances at her the wrong way suffers his wrath.

We've been so careful. She only texts me naughty photos when she knows for certain that I'm alone. She uses her friends as a cover to stay over at my place. We don't go out in public together. Mostly, we just hang out at my house and bang.

Okay, I guess that is a bit crass. We do more than just "hang out and bang." She's so funny and easy to talk to. She's great at mixing drinks, she's wicked smart, and she listens when I want to talk about hockey or motorcycles or even something personal like my fears about Matus's future.

Plus, she knows about my struggles with depression and the time I spent in a mental health facility, and yet I never feel judged or invalidated. I feel like I can show her who I really am. Slowly, I've been peeling back the layers of myself, and it hasn't scared her away. Every day, I fall harder for her.

After a few minutes, I hit the end of my run and slow the treadmill's speed to cool down. Patrick's phone rings, and I glance over to see him shutting off his machine and hopping off of it. I try not to eavesdrop, but I can tell that it's about his Make-A-Wish kid for this weekend. He sounds excited as he talks, leaning casually against the treadmill. I wonder what it's like to fulfill Wishes for kids. I'm sure he loves it, but it probably takes a lot to make sure everything goes smoothly.

When he hangs up, he smiles at me. "Did I tell you? This weekend's Wish kid chose to spend the day at Legoland Discovery Center with me. Is it weird that I am probably more excited than he is?" We both laugh together. "It will definitely beat going to Brenna's friend's wedding. You're going with Morgan in my place, right?"

"Yeah." I hit the stop button on my treadmill, and the belt comes to a rest underneath me. "Is that okay?"

"Of course," Patrick replies with a smile. Then, his face turns serious. "I'd warn you not to try anything funny with her, but of everyone on the team, I think I worry about you putting the moves on her the least."

I muster a laugh in reply but it tastes stale as it escapes my lips. At least it doesn't sound like he knows and is trying to coerce a confession from me. Not that I would tell him anything anyway.

I duck out of the workout room as quickly as I can, the weight of my secret relationship with Morgan feeling a bit heavier than usual. I hit the shower and wash up, trying to scrub the guilt off.

When I get to my phone, I have a text from Morgan asking me to call her. I wait until I'm in the car and on the road before dialing and putting it on Bluetooth. She picks up right away.

"Guess what!" Her voice is filled with excitement. I don't even have time to guess before she launches into her good news. "Steve loved my drink! He picked it over Danielle's!"

"That's awesome! You worked hard and earned it. Congratulations!"

"Thank you," she says. "And thank you again for taste-testing so many drinks for me. I couldn't have done it without your help."

"Anytime." I smile.

"Also, Steve finalized the date with the team for Matus's fundraiser at the pub. It's next weekend. They didn't want to wait for the playoff schedule to be announced, so they picked an earlier date so there won't be any conflict. I guess if Matus isn't feeling up to being there in person, we can just FaceTime him on the big TV or something."

"Is that even enough time to plan a fundraiser?" I ask.

"According to Jade, absolutely not. But the event coordinator for the team seems to think she can pull something off that isn't total ass." I can almost picture Morgan shrugging as she pauses. "I'll do whatever they need me to do to help, but I'll probably end up being behind the bar."

"It's going to go great," I assure her.

"I sure hope so," she replies.

23

MORGAN

The puck sails over the right shoulder of the goaltender and into the netting. Goal! Brenna and I hop to our feet as the goal horn blares through the arena, mixing with the sound of enthusiastic cheers celebrating Ryan's goal.

"Hell yes!" Brenna yells over the cheering and music.

"Go Velocity!" I scream with the rest of the crowd.

The air is feverish with excitement. If the Velocity win tonight's game against St. Louis, and the Philadelphia Drivers lose to Detroit, then the Velocity secure their spot in the playoffs. They've gone to the playoffs the last three years but keep getting knocked out in the first round. However, the team just keeps getting better and better, and this is going to be their year. I can just feel it.

Although, it's bittersweet. I feel the absence of Matus, and I know the guys do too. I can see it in their play at times, like when Patrick will pass the puck blindly to where Matus should be. Or when the other team wants to get scrappy and Matus isn't there to drop gloves. His absence hasn't resulted in anything more than a giveaway and a shot on goal so far, but things just aren't the same without him. Matus had surgery yesterday, so he won't be back on the ice anytime soon.

"So, where did you guys go for Carly's bachelorette party night?" I ask Brenna once things settle down and play resumes. Between her work schedule and mine, we haven't seen each other since her dress fitting last weekend.

"All over," she says. "Carly decided she wanted to start at this place near campus and then head through Uptown, but we detoured to this weird little video game bar in Logan Square." She waves her hand in the air. "I don't know. It definitely wasn't my first choice. I would have been happy chilling at Two Bits all night."

I nod absently but then notice her staring at me.

"Speaking of Two Bits, I came by after I got Carly dropped off at her place. I thought you might still be there closing, even thought it was *super* late."

I glance at the ice and then back at Brenna, unsure of where this conversation is going.

"The front door was locked up already, but some of the lights were still on in the pub."

My stomach sinks into my feet, and everything disappears from my peripheral vision.

"Oh, yeah?" I try to say casually, but it comes out as more of a strained rasp. I can't read her expression, but I'm convinced the world has stopped moving. Fuck, *fuck*. She knows. She had to have seen Nils and me.

She crinkles her nose and laughs. "You're going to laugh, but it totally looked like two people were having sex in the pub! After it was all closed up! I know I drank a lot, but I didn't think I drank *that* much." Her laughter invites me to laugh and nod along with her.

"Yeah, that's crazy," I say as smoothly as I can muster. My voice is only slightly less shaky than my hands. "You must have been more drunk than you thought."

"Probably," she says with a grin. "I mean, the blinds were wide open! I thought I saw someone's ass. I turned around, got back in the Uber, and went home since, obviously, I was white girl wasted."

"Well, I'm glad you had fun and were safe," I manage to say before we both turn our attention back to the game. Holy shit. Crisis averted. Thank you to the alcohol gods and Brenna's naïveté for keeping my secret.

I watch Nils pick at the tape on the blade of his stick while sitting on the bench during a TV timeout break. He glances up into the stands, locks eyes with me, and I see the smallest of smiles cross his face. I like him so much.

We've been so careful. Well, I mean, we've tried to be careful. It's hard to be discreet when I live with Patrick. I am either with Nils at his house, working, or home alone while the team is traveling.

Unfortunately, there is too much at stake. A slip up like that absolutely cannot happen again. I wish things could be different, but I know that Patrick would never be okay with me dating one of his teammates, especially if he found out that we'd be seeing each other secretly behind his back for several weeks.

As much as I like Nils, I need to end things with him.

Cheering pulls me from this harsh realization as the announcer shouts that Philly just lost their game against Detroit. With the Velocity up four-to-one over St. Louis and only a handful of seconds left in the game, our team will secure their spot in the playoffs.

I need to end things with Nils. But how the hell am I going to do that in the middle of a playoff run?

24

MORGAN

"I know you're not a morning person, but come on... You're coming with me this morning."

I groan and roll over, smacking my phone until it lights up with the time. "Nils, it is three-thirty in the morning. What the fuck, dude?"

He scoots over to me and trails kisses along my shoulder blade. "Please?" he begs softly. "You don't even have to get fully dressed."

How could I say no to that?

———

AT FOUR AM we arrive at Zimmerman Arena, not the practice rink, and I shoot Nils an inquisitive look as he pulls his car into a parking space. He ignores me, quickly throwing the car into park, turning it off, and getting out at lightning speed. It may not actually be lightning speed, but it certainly seems like it to my sleep-deprived brain.

I follow him in through the players' private entrance and into the locker room. He flicks the lights on, and I glance up, admiring the giant Velocity logo hanging from the ceiling. As he stops in the center of the room, it finally registers that he isn't carrying his gear.

"Uh, Nils? Did you forget something?" I ask, my voice low and scratchy from sleep.

"No," he says. "I just wanted to bring you somewhere that is special to me."

I must be missing something. "You know I've been in the locker room before, right? I'm the captain's sister, after all..."

With a soft smile, he says, "Sure, but you haven't been in this locker room with me. You haven't seen it through my eyes." He looks around, and I follow suit. The home team locker room is filled with Velocity history. Above each player's stall is a framed photo of a player from years past. Calder, Conn Smythe, and Stanley Cup champions are among the winners decorating the walls. Players I never got to meet, and a few I have. Olympians, world record holders, and people who made hockey what it is today.

"Every time I walk into this room, I see these photos and I'm reminded how lucky I am to pursue my dream. To play hockey at the highest level."

Nils takes my hand in his and leads me to the door we just came through. Gently, he turns my body so my back is against it and he's standing in front of me.

"And every time I look at you, Morgan Huff, I'm reminded how lucky I am to know you. To be able to spend time with you."

His forest-green eyes search mine. He tucks a strand of hair behind my ear and brushes his thumb along my jaw. The air hangs heavy between us, like he's looking for the words he's too nervous to say.

If he's about to get all lovey-dovey, I cannot do that right now.

If he does, that'll change everything between us.

And I can't let that happen.

"I hate that this can't be more than what it is right now, Nils. It sucks so much." Then I lean in and kiss him because talking feelings is only going to complicate things even more.

Our hands frantically pull at each other's clothes. We successfully get each other's coats off, leaving me in nothing but his baggy t-shirt and joggers that I threw on as he dragged me out the door. Through the sweats I can feel that he's rock-hard against my belly. I grind my hips against it, and he moans into my mouth at the friction.

Hungrily, he grabs my breasts in his hands, caressing them, before planting his mouth directly over one of my nipples and sucking through the thin fabric of the shirt I'm wearing. I throw my head back with a groan and hit it against the door behind me.

"Ow!" I whine, rubbing the back of my head with one hand. He laughs against my nipple, the vibrations sending waves of pleasure through me. "That really hurt!"

My other hand is fisted in his hair, and I pull on it, which only causes him to suck harder. My hips buck of their own will against him, and I quickly forget about the pain.

He leans back long enough to tug his shirt over his head, and mine quickly follows. My nipples pebble in the chilly air of the locker room. Nils presses his entire body against mine, and I welcome his body heat. Then, holding me against the door, his hands work to pull down the joggers I'm wearing. They pool on the floor at my feet. I try to step out of them, but my shoes are too big to fit through the fitted legs.

"Having issues?" He chuckles, but he kneels to help get me untangled. The moment he gets the joggers dislodged from my shoes, his hands are yanking my thong down my hips. The flimsy fabric doesn't survive his enthusiasm as I hear it snap.

"Really?" I sigh. "Again?"

"I wouldn't keep breaking them if you'd just stop wearing them in the first place," Nils growls against my inner thigh. His tongue darts out and licks the tender skin there, tracing a line up and toward my center. I whine in anticipation.

"Such a pretty pussy," he murmurs.

"You're a tease," I whimper.

"You like it," he replies with a wicked grin.

He captures my sensitive clit in his mouth, and the sound that involuntarily leaves my mouth is something close to a scream. His tongue caresses it as he slides his hand around the back of my thigh, teasing my opening with his fingers. My legs are already trembling, and I can feel a bead of sweat racing down my back. The way this man worships my body...

Two fingers enter me at once, and I cry out again from the intense pleasure. My body moves on its own, riding his face and his hand in search of my release. I can feel it getting closer and closer with every thrust.

"Not so fast," Nils says, pulling away. The sudden loss of contact has all my nerves on end. I need more.

He rises to his feet and grabs my butt, pulling me upward to him. I wrap my legs around his waist as he guides his cock to my entrance. Eagerly, I sink onto it, and we both groan. Fuck, I will never get tired of how he feels inside me.

The rocking of his hips against mine pushes my back against the door with a satisfying *thunk* over and over. My legs are trembling, and my breathing is erratic. I look into his eyes, and I see the same primal need that I feel.

I can't fight my climax any longer, and I fall apart in his arms. He thrusts through it, following me over the edge shortly after. Panting, we hold onto each other, both savoring every last moment of our shared orgasm.

Gently, he pulls out, and I climb off of him. We're both coated in sweat. "Ready to hit the showers?" he asks, his smile a mile wide. He grabs shampoo, body wash, and a towel from his stall and hands them to me. "You get started, and I'll be in there in a minute."

I walk into the massive shower room, pick one of the stalls, and turn on the water. It doesn't take long for it to warm up, and I step in, letting the water cascade over my shoulders and down my body. It feels great on my muscles, which I can tell will be a little sore from this tryst.

I'm putting his woodsy-scented shampoo in my hair when Nils finally comes in. He quickly steps into the shower, and I'm instantly on high alert. His face is white, his lips in a tense line.

"What's wrong?" I ask him over the sound of the water.

"Patrick is here."

It feels like the warm water turns to ice. "*What?*"

"He *heard* us. He doesn't know it was you, though." Nils runs a hand through his hair. "He asked me if it was good and fist-bumped me in congratulations."

If only he knew it was me that Nils was fucking. Also, ew, I can't believe my brother heard us. "Where is he now?"

"In the athletic training room," Nils says. "He said he has an early session with the strength coach. So, we need to get out of here before he comes back down."

"Fuck," I say. "Let me get the shampoo out of my hair. Can you get my clothes?"

"Yeah." He steps out of the shower to get my stuff. I've never rinsed so fast in my entire life. When I turn off the water, Nils is there with our clothes.

"I grabbed one of the extra hoodies from my stall for you," he says quickly. "Put it on and pull the hood up. Hopefully, we won't see him, but just in case, it will help you blend in." We pull our clothing on as quickly as we can while listening for any sign of Patrick. Thankfully, we manage to get dressed and out of there unseen.

Nils grabs my hand and pulls me down the darkened hallway toward the exit. We don't stop running until we're safely in his car. He wastes no time throwing it into gear and pulling out of the parking lot.

"That was close," he says as we drive away.

"Too close," I say under my breath.

25

NILS

"Looking good, lady killer," Matus says with a toothy grin. I FaceTimed him to check out my suit for the wedding. He's been feeling a bit better since the surgery, and I know he's missing us, so I want him to feel included as much as I can.

A large section of his face is covered in gauze and tape. The parts of his skin that I can see are largely swollen and bruised. He somehow looks worse than before. But he is in good spirits today. Maybe it's the Vicodin talking.

"Too bad you won't be at the wedding tonight; I was looking forward to seeing you in a velvet suit," I quip at him.

"Velvet!" he exclaims. "You know I'd rock the fuck out of a velvet suit. Hey, I wonder if they make velvet hospital gowns."

I hold my phone in one hand and brush a fuzz off the lapel of my jacket with the other hand. The entire suit is a solid, dark burgundy color, including the vest underneath. I paired it with a black dress shirt and a burgundy floral tie. Every item is tailored to fit me perfectly. Of course, as a hockey player, I own many tailored suits, but I bought this one specifically because I wanted to impress Morgan. I hope she likes it.

Morgan looks absolutely drop-dead gorgeous when Ryan and I pick her up for the wedding. She's wearing a dark green halter gown that hugs every curve and showcases her cleavage with a plunging neckline. Her hair is in waves, and her makeup makes her gold-colored eyes pop.

Maybe wearing ultra-fitted pants wasn't the best idea today.

Ryan insisted we get a limo so the three of us – plus Brenna, who is already at the venue with the bride – didn't need to worry about driving home, but I think he also just wanted to flex a bit to impress Carly's and John's friends.

I've heard bits and pieces from Morgan about the weird power dynamic between Brenna and Carly, and I wonder if the limo is part of it. It doesn't sound like the healthiest of friendships.

Since our playoff spot is locked in, we're all breathing a bit easier. I'm looking forward to a few days of fun and relaxation before the playoff run begins after next weekend.

Ryan grabs a bottle of champagne and pops the cork. Morgan hands me champagne flutes from the cabinet next to her seat. I hold them out for Ryan to fill and then distribute them.

"To a great evening with great friends," he says, and we all clink our glasses together with a resounding, "Cheers!"

Morgan pulls out her phone and selects the first song from a playlist called, "I Make Pour Decisions." Immediately, she and Ryan start shouting along. The ride passes quickly as they sing and dance to songs that were popular here in North America when they were younger. I recognize a few of them between them being played in various hockey arenas or from bars or clubs I've been to. Morgan knows the words to almost every tune, and Ryan seems to know a lot of them too. Luckily, I'm content to sit back, sipping champagne, and enjoy the moment with my friends.

Well, my friend and my more-than-friend, I guess. It doesn't roll off the tongue very well.

The wedding ceremony is held at an old church and thankfully doesn't drag on for an eternity. Ryan, Morgan, and I are seated much closer to the front than Morgan expected, based on her comments to Ryan about wedding seating and etiquette. I suppose with a wedding planner for a best friend, you know the rules of these things, but it's all foreign to me. I spend most of the ceremony trying not to stare at Morgan's tits.

We see Brenna in the receiving line, another foreign concept to me, and she quickly tells us some of the drama from before the ceremony, including a bridesmaid busting the zipper on her dress and it being held together with safety pins, two of the groomsmen showing up already drunk, and the photographer mistaking John's dad for his grandfather during pre-ceremony family photos. I glance down the line at the parents. John's father looks older than I expected, so I can see how the photographer might mess that up.

Soon enough, Brenna and the rest of the bridal party are getting into their limousine to go take more photos. Ryan, Morgan, and I get into our limo and head to the reception, which is being held at a mansion in one of the suburbs.

Music is playing, hors d'oeuvres are being served, and drinks are flowing from the open bar when we arrive. I head to the bar to grab drinks for the three of us while Ryan greets a few of John's friends and Morgan heads to the bathroom. After signing an autograph for someone at the bar, I head back with drinks in hand to our table.

"Thanks, Nils!" Ryan says as he takes the glass of French 75 from my hand. His cheeks are flushed from the multiple glasses of champagne we had on the way over. "Have you met Janice and Rodger?"

"I haven't," I say. "Um, nice to meet you." Absently, I shake hands with each of them. I think they're Carly's parents, but I'm keeping an eye on the door, awaiting Morgan's return. As if on cue, she comes walking in, carrying herself with an air of confidence.

I give up on trying not to stare and finally allow my gaze to rake over her as she approaches. She locks eyes with me, and a smirk crosses her face. Busted.

Pretending to be just friends with her has already been excruciating. But keeping up the ruse tonight might be the death of me.

26

MORGAN

Nils being my date feels like torture. He looks handsome as hell in a dark red suit, his blond hair slicked back, and the scruffy beginnings of a playoff beard on his face. But being this close to him is hard as hell. I keep catching myself staring at him while thinking about where I'd love to feel that scruff on my body or reaching toward him to tousle his hair and stopping myself. When we're hanging out at his house, we touch and kiss all we want without any worries.

I need to be careful. And I need to end things... eventually. I feel my resolve waning as the days pass. I'm just so comfortable with Nils. I get to be myself with him, and the sex is mind-blowing. It's like he knows every inch of my body by heart.

Shaking my head slightly, I try to bring my focus

back to the speech John's best man is giving from the table next to us.

Carly and John went for a bit of a non-traditional seating arrangement for the head table. They are the only people *at* the head table, as if Carly is afraid that people will be looking at someone other than her or something. Their bridal party is spread out among the guest tables positioned near the head table. This allows for Brenna to be seated with Ryan, Nils, and me. We're at a table with another bridesmaid and her boyfriend, but I quickly forgot their names.

The best man's poor attempt at a funny speech finally ends, and our table clinks our glasses together and drink to his toast. Then, Brenna takes the microphone from him and stands, looking a little nervous. She and Ryan trade a glance, communicating wordlessly, and I watch it boost her confidence. I try to focus on her speech and not on the surge of jealousy I'm feeling... because I wish I could share a moment like that with Nils.

"I tried to write a speech for days about what Carly means to me and how great John is for her, but nothing sounded quite right," Brenna begins. "So, I guess I'm just going to wing it."

The girls share a smile before Brenna begins to speak directly to her. "Carly, you and I have been through everything together. From frat parties and shitty professors, to late night talks and thrift store adventures, to our dumpy little house and my stalker ex-boyfriend, to now... I think the only thing more constant than us, is you and John."

She turns to him. "John, I knew from the moment I first met you that you and Carly were the real deal. Your relationship gave me hope when I had given up on love." Brenna smiles at Ryan before turning back to John. "You showed me that everyone deserves a happily ever after. You both showed me that love is out there, and it is respectful and kind and funny and full of joy."

I bite my lip to keep the tears at bay.

"To Mr. and Mrs. Hewitt," she says, raising her champagne flute, and we all follow suit. "May tonight make it into your social media year in review highlight reel. Cheers."

We clink glasses again and take a drink as Brenna sits back down, looking as choked up as I feel. Ryan grabs her face and pulls her into a steamy kiss over their glasses of champagne, and with envy, I watch him squeeze her bare thigh under the hem of her short dress. I don't want to be jealous of her, but I can't help it. I want public displays of affection so freaking bad.

The DJ starts the music back up, and people begin to dance and mingle. I don't notice it, though. I'm stuck inside my own head.

I want what John and Carly have – what Ryan and Brenna have. I want to be loved wildly and with abandon. I want to be consumed by it. I want it to course through my veins every moment of every day, a fire that never dies down but only grows bigger over time.

I feel Nils's hand on my shoulder. "Care to dance?" he asks with a kind smile, and my heart races.

I *do* have it. I have what Carly and John have. Fuck, the love Nils shows me is funny and kind and all the other things Brenna said.

I'm in love with him.

"I need some air," I somehow manage to say as I push past him out the doors and into the night.

27

NILS

Something's wrong. The way Morgan bolted has me quickly following behind her, dodging other partygoers with drinks in their hands as I move.

"Morgan, wait," I call out to her as we reach the curved driveway in front of the mansion. In the distance, several concierge drivers watching us, but I'm not concerned about them. I finally catch up to her as she turns to face me. "*Min kära,* what's wrong?"

I've never seen her cry before, but her eyes are filled with tears, threatening to spill down her cheeks and ruin her makeup. The expression on her face breaks my heart. She opens her mouth to try and speak, but no words come out.

I pull her into a hug, and her arms wrap around my waist, pulling me in tightly to her. She shivers slightly under the late winter air, and I rub my hands over her bare shoulders to warm them.

Eventually, she releases her grip on me a bit, and we pull back from each other to lock eyes.

"I'm sick of having to hide us," she says. "I am sick of having to hide how happy you make me. It just sucks watching everyone else hug and kiss and touch each other. I only get to steal glances at you, and that just isn't enough. I am sick of having to keep us a damn secret because of what Patrick would think about it. Screw that, I want to love you like that. I want all of that with you."

I don't know who initiates it, but our lips collide. We both know the stakes, but our hearts clearly haven't gotten the memo. There is so much passion in this kiss, so many emotions. I want her to know I want this too, but it is a risk. Not just a little risk, but a my-whole-career risk. Yet, as I cup her face in my hand and pull her body against mine, it all fades away. She is worth all of the risks. I want this too.

"*What the fuck?*"

The blood drains from every inch of my body, and we violently rip apart from each other, turning to face Patrick. He's only partially illuminated by the old-fashioned streetlamps lining the drive, but I can still feel the rage emanating off of him.

"I-I can explain," Morgan stammers, placing a protective hand over my stomach.

"Nils," he growls, voice low. I'm frozen, unable to move or speak. "What the *hell* is going on?"

"It isn't what it looks like!" Morgan exclaims, which only serves to piss Patrick off even more.

"Shut up." He stalks toward us, and I feel actual fear pass through my body. I could probably outrun him. I honestly consider trying. "How long?" We're both silent, and he asks again as he slowly approaches us, "How long has... *this*... been going on?"

Morgan and I exchange a glance, reconciling the potential consequences of telling the truth. I finally speak, "A few weeks."

"*A few weeks*," Patrick repeats after me, his words dripping with venom. "Are you fucking kidding me?" I watch him put the pieces together in his head. "It was her. She's the girl I heard you with at the arena the other day. What the fuck? That's my *sister*."

He is standing in front of us now. Morgan is still between Patrick and me, guarding me. Patrick would never hurt his sister, but I am a different story.

"What are you even doing here?" Morgan asks, possibly in an attempt to distract him from murdering me. "I thought you were with the Make-A-Wish kid."

"He was tired from the chemo, so we had to call it quits early," he manages to spit out, still fuming. "I thought I would drop by the wedding and enjoy the party. I never thought I'd catch my teammate playing tonsil hockey with my sister."

"Patrick—"

"Stop. Just stop. I don't want to hear anything you have to say."

"Goddamn it, that's not fair!"

Patrick holds a hand up in her face. "I don't give two shits about what you think is fair right now. You know what's not fair? You getting involved with one of my teammates. You know how messy that will be when you two break up? You know how bad it makes me look to the owners that the captain's sister is sleeping with one of his teammates?"

Morgan grabs his hand and pushes it back down to his side. "I knew you'd blow up like this."

"And yet you went and hooked up with him anyway. You're ridiculous."

"Fuck you!" Morgan attempts to shove him, but he easily holds his place. In one quick move, he pushes her to the side and takes a swing at my head. Thankfully, I anticipate it and duck, feeling his fist brush the top of my hair.

Morgan loses her balance and falls to the pavement with a yelp, but I'm distracted as Patrick takes a second swing that I don't anticipate quite as well. His fist connects with my jaw, and pain rockets through my skull.

Before I can get a swing in of my own, someone bigger than me is pulling Patrick away. I stumble back, watching Brenna help Morgan back to her feet and Ryan restraining Patrick. My jaw throbs. Thankfully, the punch he landed was with his off-hand or else I'd probably be unconscious right now.

"Fuck you both," Patrick yells as Ryan half-drags him down the driveway to his car. "You're fucking dead to me, Nils Larsson!"

Brenna and Morgan retreat into the mansion, leaving me outside with a few nosy onlookers. I run my thumb over the lump forming on my jaw before deciding to call myself an Uber. This night, my career, and whatever Morgan and I had are all likely over.

28

MORGAN

"You can't hide from your brother forever," Jade says as she hands me a steaming coffee mug. I gratefully accept it from her and concentrate on scooping sugar into the mug. "Morgan."

"I know," I say with a sigh, stirring my coffee until the sugar dissolves. I take a seat at Jade's dining room table across from her and glance out the window. The sun is high in the sky already, its bright rays reflecting off the snow, causing me to squint.

After Ryan stepped in to stop Pat from killing Nils, and Brenna took me inside and made sure I wasn't hurt from falling down, I took an Uber to the airport and got on the first plane to Minneapolis with nothing but the dress I was wearing at the wedding. Jade answered my call in the middle of the night and drove from the hotel she was staying at in Mankato for the bridal show to pick me up at the airport. She then loaned me an oversized t-shirt and let me sleep in her bed as late as I needed.

"Have you talked to Nils yet?"

Nils. I still can't believe Patrick caught us making out. I can't believe they got into a fist fight because of a kiss. I can't believe we probably upstaged Carly's wedding... Can't wait to hear about *that* later.

This is even worse than what I thought would ever happen if Patrick found out. As protective as I know my brother is, I never thought he would take things to this extreme.

"No," I finally say after taking a sip of coffee. "I haven't checked my phone yet this morning, though."

"I can't believe Patrick decked him," Jade says, then she backtracks, "I mean, I can believe it since this isn't the first guy he's punched because of you. But still. Nils seems so nice and harmless."

"I think that's *why* Patrick is so pissed. He never expected Nils to be a person he needed to worry about."

Jade tilts her head thoughtfully as she listens, some of her long black braids falling to the side. "I've known you both for a long time. I know your brother loves you, but... this is not okay. He can't continue to be this overprotective father figure. You're a grown woman, who can make your own decisions."

I stare at the ceiling and sigh. "I know. But... you also know that he takes that role seriously."

"I know." Jade grabs my hand from across the table. "But his endearing protectiveness has moved into straight up scary territory. This isn't healthy for any of you."

A bright red Cardinal lands on the bird feeder outside the window.

"Your brother cannot be your keeper. It isn't fair to you or him, and it especially isn't fair to Nils." Jade runs her thumb across the top of my hand as I continue to watch the Cardinal out the window. "I know Patrick is just looking to keep you safe because he couldn't save your dad, but he shouldn't be projecting that onto you. Your dad would want you to be with a good man, and Nils *is* a good man. He would approve of Nils, and you know it."

"I'm in love with him," I say softly as the red bird and I stare at each other. Jade squeezes my hand. "And I think he loves me, too." I realize now that he was spilling his heart to me that morning in the locker room, but I wasn't ready to hear it and shut him down.

The Cardinal ruffles his feathers, the sunshine highlighting their brilliant red hue.

"Do you see yourself having a future with him?"

"Absolutely," I blurt out. I'm as sure of that as I am that this winged visitor is trying to tell me something.

"Is he worth the risk of losing the close relationship you have with your brother?"

I watch the Cardinal run the feathers on his side through his beak, cleaning them one by one. It's such a deliberate act of self-care, to make sure each one is perfectly washed and put it back in its place. As I watch, I think back to Brenna's maid of honor speech and remember her describing love as respectful, kind, and full of joy. Nils is all of those things to me and even more.

I need to choose the love I deserve.

"Yeah, he is."

We're both quiet, lost in thought. The Cardinal launches itself into the air and flies away.

Thanks, Dad, I think to myself. He would have loved Nils.

When Dad died, my life paused. I fell out of touch with most of my friends. I never went back to school after I failed out, and I took the first job I found. It's lucky that I love Two Bits, but it's time for me to aim higher.

"Jade?"

"Yeah?"

"Do you think it would be crazy if I went back to school?"

"Depends on what you want to major in," she says,

leaning back in her chair. "I don't think you can study mortuary sciences at a state school."

I stick my tongue out at her. "I know I dress like Wednesday Addams, but I think I want to go back for business."

"Business? Why's that?"

"I want to make something of myself. I don't want to spend the rest of my life riding Patrick's coattails. A business degree would give me a range of job opportunities. And I already have so much experience from working behind the scenes with the Velocity. When my name is on that diploma, the sky is the limit. It will be the start of my own legacy."

Jade smiles softly. "What made you decide now is the time?"

"Nils," I answer truthfully. "He is so driven. When he knows what he wants, he goes after it as quickly as he can. He doesn't let anything hold him back or slow him down. After spending the last few years just coasting, I'm ready to go fast."

29

NILS

My entire body is sore from riding so many miles on my bike today. I hopped on it as soon as the sun came up and have only stopped for gas and piss breaks over the last six hours. But the distraction of the ride has numbed the pain in my jaw while simultaneously numbing the pain in my heart.

I know I'm using the bike to try to escape. On or off the ice, speed makes me forget. It makes me feel invincible, or at least like nothing can hurt me.

I stop at a decrepit gas station on the side of the highway to fill up and check my phone for the first time in over a hundred miles. The GPS tells me I'm on the far side of Iowa, almost to Nebraska, which I could have guessed based on the lack of any scenery besides giant, empty fields. My phone tells me that Matus called, and Morgan tried calling again. I haven't been able to bring myself to have a conversation with her yet.

The phone feels heavy in my hand. I place it on the seat of my bike so I can take off my helmet. My hair is all over the place, but I don't care. I've been sweating something fierce, even though it's still almost too cold to ride. Grabbing my phone from the seat, I carry it with my helmet into the gas station. My stomach rumbles, and now that I'm off the bike, I can't blame it on the turbulence of the roads. I guess it's time to resort to gas station grub.

After I grab a drink, a couple of shriveled hot dogs that look like they've been on the rollers for a week, and a bag of chips from the convenience store, I sit down in a small dining area for the truck drivers. My trainer would kill me if he saw me eating this greasy garbage. Yet another thing I try not to think about. Good thing we have a week off before playoffs start.

I am aware I'm avoiding calling Morgan back. It's not her fault, and I don't blame her for Patrick's actions. I played with fire, and I got burned. I am not used to having something to lose and someone I care about. And by avoiding that inevitable conversation, I've been hanging on to hope. But enough is enough. I need to stop running from her when all I want is to run *to* her. So, I pull my phone out of my pocket and take a deep breath as I click her name in my contacts.

She picks up on the first ring. "Hey."

"Hey," I say back.

"How are you? How is your face?"

"I'm fine. How are you?"

"I'm okay," she says.

A pause, then, "So..."

"So..." She matches me. There's another awkward pause. "I'm so sorry."

"It's fine," I tell her, staring at my bike out the window. "I completely understand. There are no hard feelings. We had fun, but I know ending things is what is best."

"Wait, what?" Her voice sounds confused and slightly panicked.

"That's why you've been calling me, right? Because we need to end things?"

The line is quiet for a moment, before she asks, "Is that what you want?"

I'm caught a bit off-guard. "I thought that's what you wanted. I mean, your brother..."

"Nils, I..." Her voice trails off. "I don't want to end things."

My heart skips a beat. "Y-you don't? But what about—"

"What about him?" she interjects. "I guess I'm going to say something, and if you don't feel the same, then just tell me and we can end things." She takes a breath, and I can picture her clearly in my mind, relaxing her shoulders on the exhale as she builds her resolve. "I like you. A lot. And I'm done hiding my feelings for you from everyone in order to protect my brother. I don't give a fuck what he thinks anymore. I'm ready to be reckless and wild, and I want a love that makes me *feel*. There's so much I haven't been able to experience. But I want to do those things with you. I want you to keep making my heart skip beats. I want all of you... that is, if you want me too."

"Is this really a good idea?" I watch a family get out of their van, the youngest kid staring at my motorcycle with wide eyes as they walk into the gas station. "I don't want to cause trouble for Patrick or the team."

"I understand your hesitation, and I respect you for it. I think we've both been hesitant to get too invested because of all the extra crap, the what ifs. We've been thinking of everyone *except* us." Her voice is calm, even, and confident, like she prepared for my rebuttal and has responses ready. "But I'm also telling you this: I am all in and ready to face them if you are. I'm ready to choose us. You just have to say yes."

With my free hand, I grab my riding gloves and helmet. "Where are you right now?"

"Uh, Minneapolis." She's caught off-guard. "Why?"

"How soon can you be back to Chicago?" I push open the door and head outside toward my bike.

"I mean, I could probably head to the airport right now, book a standby seat for a flight, and hopefully end up on one for later tonight. But there's no guarantee of getting on one."

Dissatisfied, I grunt, "hang on," and open up the maps application on my phone. It would take just as long for me to drive straight to her as it would to meet her in Chicago. I bring the phone back up to my ear. "Text me the address where you are. I will be there in six hours, give or take."

"Uh... What?" I hear the hesitation in Morgan's voice. "You're coming here? Where are you?"

"Somewhere near the edge of Iowa and Nebraska. You just have to say yes," I echo her words back to her as I reach the bike. "I'll see you soon, *min kära*."

Her reply is drowned out by the throaty sound of the engine coming to life. I hang up and stuff my phone back into my pocket. It'll be a long trip across Iowa and Minnesota, but my body doesn't feel nearly as sore now that my heart is being put back together.

30

MORGAN

It's dark and bitterly cold outside when a single headlight finally pulls into Jade's driveway. The butterflies in my stomach have been violently trying to escape for the last six hours, banging around inside me, causing havoc and unrest.

I didn't realize how badly I needed to see Nils. My soul ached for him. And now, I'm finally standing in front of him again, watching as he pulls the helmet off his head, that mop of blond hair sticking up in every direction, and I can't hear anything except my heartbeat. Luckily, we don't need words. We embrace with the tightest of squeezes under the chilly night sky, putting every ounce of pain from the last twenty-four hours into the gesture.

A shiver snaps me back to reality. If we don't go inside soon, we might freeze to death. And he drove too damn far to die of hypothermia in Jade's front yard, so I pull away a little bit.

"It is way too cold out here. Let's go inside." I lead him up the drive and into Jade's house. Nils places his helmet, driving gloves, jacket, and boots on the bench in the foyer, and we head into the living room.

Jade and Nils have crossed paths at Velocity games and events, but they've never properly been introduced. Nils extends a hand to shake hers, but she pulls him into a friendly hug instead. "I feel like I already know you," she says with a laugh. "It's nice to finally meet you."

"Likewise." He smiles.

"I'll give you two some space to talk," she says to us and leaves the room with a gentle wave as I take a seat on the couch.

Nils sits in the armchair adjacent to where I am, turning to face me. He's wearing black jeans and a fitted maroon sweater, and his hair is still a mess. I lean forward and run my hands through it, attempting to get it back into place, but it refuses to cooperate, and I give up. He looks exhausted, and his jaw is starting to bruise, but I'm so glad he's here.

"I fucking missed you," I tell him.

"I missed you too." He reaches out for me, and I meet him halfway. He affectionately rubs his thumb across the back of my hand. "How do we make this work?"

"I think I need to sit down and talk to Patrick first. He won't murder me, so I think I can face a lot of the hard questions without him being as heated as he would be with you. Then, we need to sit down and have a conversation with him together. And if he can't accept the fact that we want to be together, then..." I trail off. The thought of my brother being angry at me hurts so much, but the thought of losing Nils hurts even more.

"I'm all in if you are," he says. Our eyes meet, and I'm reminded of that day at the bowling alley when he gently guided my throw to help me improve. Then, I remember the countless drinks he taste-tested to help me create the perfect cocktail. He is always helping me be better than I was before and cheering for me. I am so used to cheering for other people that having someone root for me and my dreams feels surreal. How did I get so lucky?

"I love you," I say breathlessly.

The corners of his eyes crinkle when he smiles. "I love you too."

———

WE SPEND Monday exploring Minneapolis after we drop by the mall to pick up some clothes for Nils since he arrived with nothing but himself and his bike. We also pick up a helmet for me, since mine is at his house in Chicago. Then I show him my old stomping grounds, including driving past Mom's house. I'm just not ready to tell her what happened between Patrick, Nils, and me. I assume Patrick hasn't told her either because I would have heard from her by now. Someday soon, I hope to be able to introduce her to Nils as my boyfriend.

On Tuesday, Nils is finally feeling recovered enough to start the ride back to Chicago. I promise Jade that I'll see her on Saturday when she flies in for Matus's fundraiser event. She waves goodbye from her front door as we pull away on the motorcycle. It's cold, and I'm not used to riding for long stretches, so we plan to take our time getting back to Chicago, enjoying the scenery and our time together.

We stop in La Crosse, Wisconsin for the evening and see the World's Largest Six-Pack, which are beer brewing tanks painted to look like a six-pack of beer. We also head up to Granddad Bluff, and although it is blustery, Nils places his coat over my shoulder as we enjoy the view of the city nestled in the valley.

On Wednesday, we cruise east across Wisconsin to the Wisconsin Dells. We visit the Ripley's Believe It or

Not Museum, and we giggle our way through it, getting lost in the hidden passageways and stealing kisses from each other every moment we can. Nils takes me to a place with hundreds of tame whitetail deer, and we spend the evening petting them.

On Thursday, we arrive in Milwaukee. Nils insists that we go to the Harley-Davidson Museum, and I happily oblige. I find myself looking at him, wide-eyed and in awe like a kid in a candy store, more than the motorcycles. We eat tacos in a restaurant made from converted Airstream RVs and stand on the shore of Lake Michigan until the sun goes down.

On Friday, we arrive back in the Windy City as the sun is rising. As the skyline comes into view, glass and metal coming out of the haze, I start to feel nervous. The week Nils and I spent together cruising the northern Midwest was absolutely magical. It's been nice to spend time together out in the open and not have to hide. It's also been a nice distraction from what awaits us when we get home.

I haven't spoken to Patrick at all since he caught us at the wedding. He hasn't tried contacting me either, but Jade had let him know I came to her place and that I was safe. If he was really worried, he would have reached out.

Nils and I arrive in front of the building where Patrick and I live. I hop off the bike and remove my helmet, running my free hand through my hair to tame it slightly. Nils opens the visor on his helmet, and I give him a quick kiss.

"Tell Matus I say hi and congratulations on finally busting out of the hospital," I say.

"I will," he says. "Please keep me updated, and call me if anything happens."

"I'll be okay," I promise him. The bruising on his jaw is finally starting to subside, although it is currently obscured by his helmet. "I love you."

"I love you too." He flips his visor down, and I lean in, tapping my forehead and his helmet together as I take a deep, steadying breath. As I pull back, he revs the bike. With a throaty growl from the engine, he pulls away and disappears into traffic.

31

MORGAN

I cautiously open the door to the condo and notice how messy it is. The kitchen counter is littered with bottles, cans, and presumably empty take-out containers. There is a pile of dirty clothes sitting in the middle of the living room, and next to it is Patrick, who is eyeing me warily. I set my motorcycle helmet, riding gloves, and purse on the end table as I come into the room.

"Hey," I say.

Patrick scoffs.

"You didn't call me at all," I reply.

"You didn't call either," he retorts.

"I didn't think you'd want to hear from me," I say, sinking into the armchair across from him.

"You're right about that." His words are still tinged

with sharpness, and his body language remains guarded.

I sigh. "Patrick, I'm sorry. I never wanted you to find out like that. I never even wanted to be involved with a hockey player, especially not someone on the team. But..."

"It just happened?" he offers sarcastically.

"Yeah," I say with a shrug.

"How long has this been going on?"

"Since Matus's injury," I tell him truthfully.

He brushes a hand across his already-impressive dark playoff beard. "At least I haven't been oblivious for like, a year or something."

"No, definitely not," I reassure him. "I promise, it hasn't been long at all. And I felt bad the entire time. I was even going to end things with him, but then the team made the playoffs..."

"And now?"

I glance at my hands in my lap and brace myself. "Well, I love him. And he feels the same about me."

I hear Patrick exhale, but I can't bring myself to look at him. A pin-pricking sensation covers my skin, and my muscles are tense.

"I've only ever tried to protect you," he says in a soft tone. I muster the courage to look at him and find him staring out the window. "If I've been too overbearing, I truly am sorry."

"You have been, but I get it. I accept your apology," I reply. "I know Dad left huge shoes to fill, and I'm so thankful for you being there for me."

"I wanted to make him proud," he says. We finally make eye contact. "He loved you more than you can even imagine."

"I'm sure you make him proud every single day, Pat. I know you do."

After a brief but meaningful pause, he says, "So, what happens now?"

"Well, Nils wants to have a conversation with you too. But we plan to continue seeing each other. If you aren't okay with that, I can move out and he will request a trade, so you don't even have to be on the same team anymore." I take a breath. "But that isn't what he or I want, and I hope it isn't what you want either, although I understand if it is. We snuck around behind your back and lied to you for weeks, and we are both very sorry for it. I hope you can forgive both of us someday."

"Come here," he says to me, standing up. I rise, and he engulfs me in an unexpected bear hug. It feels a bit strange since he's much taller than Nils and a bit more muscular, but I also can't remember the last time we hugged like this. It feels nice. "I can't promise to love it, and I definitely don't want to hear any details, but I forgive you, and I am so happy you found someone that I don't absolutely fucking hate."

I smile into his shirt, trying to ignore the fact that it smells like sweat from his morning workout.

"If you want to move out and live with Nils, I understand, but please don't let him request a trade. The team needs him next year, and so do I."

We finally let go of each other. "You can't get rid of me that easily." I glance around at the trash and filth everywhere. "Obviously, you still need my help around here."

Patrick grabs my head under one arm and rubs his knuckles over my scalp in an affectionate noogie. I laugh and manage to worm myself away from him.

"Love you, Morgs."

"Love you too, Pat."

EPILOGUE

Matus gingerly steps out of the car in front of Two Bits, blinking against the harsh sun. I toss the keys to the valet driver as Morgan grabs the door for us. He's only been out of the hospital for two days, but, "If they're throwing a party with my name on it, then of course I'm going to be there," is what he said to me yesterday. So, here he is.

A large bandage still covers most of one side of his face, but he smiles as best as he can for the cameras as we step inside the pub. The team's event coordinators worked all week with the staff of Two Bits to make the pub look amazing for the fundraiser. Extra lighting, tables and chairs, and some classy, Velocity-themed decor have really perked up the place.

A couple other guys from the team wave Matus over. As he peels away, I reach back, taking Morgan's hand in mine and lead her to a table near the bar, where Ryan and Brenna are already sitting.

"Look at you two!" Ryan says loudly, a huge grin on his face. "Who would have ever seen that one coming?"

"Congratulations," Brenna says much more serenely. "You guys are really cute together."

"You have got to tell me the whole story of how this happened," says Ryan. "And how you avoided certain death by Patrick."

"Maybe someday," I say, smiling at Morgan. She beams back at me, looking even more radiant than usual. Maybe it's the happiness and the relief that we don't have to hide anymore that are making her glow today.

"Morgan!" Steve yells at her from the kitchen doorway. He's wearing a dirty apron over a dress shirt and slacks. I've never seen him dressed up before, but it's no surprise that he's also working. Morgan pulls me over to him, and I can feel eyes on us as we move across the room. I squeeze her hand a little harder. "I'm so glad you both are back."

"Thanks for being so understanding, Steve," she says.

"How could I not be?" he replies. "You've taken maybe two days off the entire time you've worked here. And the fact that you ran off on a romantic motorcycle tour of the Midwest? You know I'm a sucker for a good love story."

"You big softy," Morgan says with a grin.

Steve glances over us at the room filled with drinks and chatter. He focuses back on Morgan, and his demeanor changes. "Hey, I wanted to float something past ya if you have a second."

"Sure. What's on your mind?"

He clears his throat. He's nervous, and so am I. "You know I'm getting older, and Danielle has no interest in the family business. If you're interested in taking her over, I'd love to pass on the reins of Two Bits to you."

I swear, her jaw hits the floor. "*What*? Steve, I-I can't," she stammers. "First of all, I don't know jack shit about running a restaurant, and secondly, you know I can't afford to buy the place."

A smile crosses his face, and he glances at me. "You don't have to worry. I'll teach you everything you need to know. I wouldn't just leave you high and dry. What kind of guy do you think I am? As for finances..."

I clear my throat. "Patrick and I agreed to go in on it together. We'll be your primary investors. And Patrick said that once you're stable and turning a good enough profit, he'd be happy to sell his stake in it to you."

"You're joking. You've got to be kidding." She

looks back and forth between Steve and me, jaw dropped, before glancing over at Patrick across the room. Patrick looks up from the conversation he's having, and with a soft smile, raises his glass in our direction.

That night in the kitchen when it was just Steve and I, he mentioned the idea of Morgan taking over the restaurant. In between flipping burgers and garnishing plates, we talked about what it might take to make it happen. And I had my first conversation with Patrick about it before everything went down. Things are still awkward between us, and probably will be for a while, but I think we've both come to an understanding that we want what's best for Morgan – whatever it requires from either of us. And then, Jade told me how Morgan was talking about going back to school for business, and the pieces all started to fall into place.

"This is real if you want it," I say to her. "Of course, you can say no."

"We all would understand and support you either way," Steve says. "But we all have seen your passion, and we believe in you. You love this place more than anyone. You'll take care of her and treat her right. And really, I need a fucking break." He lets out a huge laugh that we can't help but join in on.

"Okay, but... I was hoping to go back to school—"

Steve cuts her off. "I'll stay on and manage things until you get your degree," he says, and I think I sense a hint of pride in his voice. "Nothing will change until you're ready for them to. We want Two Bits to help you achieve your dreams, not hold you back from them. She'll be ready for you when you're ready for her."

Morgan's eyes focus out the window beside us, and light up. I follow her gaze and see a bright red Cardinal sitting on the sidewalk. She's choked up, but says, "Dad says yes. Fuck it. Let's do this." She grabs my hand, and we shake, then she does the same with Steve. "You have yourselves a deal."

Applause erupts across the bar as a bunch of the team cheers for Morgan. I might have told Patrick to let them in on it. I wanted her to feel supported, and I think I succeeded. She's glowing.

"Next round is on me!" she yells out. The entire place erupts into cheers. Then she turns to me, "Well, it's on you. I don't have that kind of money."

"You think I do? I just bought a bar. I'm broke!" We both laugh as I wrap my arm around her waist, leading her over to a table with Brenna, Ryan, Patrick, and Jade.

"Congratulations!" Brenna says cheerfully as we take a seat.

"You were all in on it?" Morgan asks them. They all grin and nod.

"Well, some of us more than others," Patrick tells her. I notice that his arm is wrapped around Jade's shoulder.

Morgan notices it too, and her eyes go wide. "What is happening here?" she demands, pointing a finger back and forth at them. Patrick cringes, and Jade blushes.

"Oh boy, that's quite the story," Ryan jumps in. "Your friends here got themselves into quite an interesting situation."

"And that situation is..." Morgan asks.

Jade leans in closer to Morgan and me and drops her voice. "Please just go along with it, Morgs."

"Go along with what!?"

"Your genius brother got tired of Danielle coming over here to hit on him. He told her that he has a girlfriend," Ryan informs us gleefully. "And when Danielle asked who she is, he panicked and said the first name that came to his head... Jade."

My jaw drops open. Patrick looks like he'd rather be anywhere but here right now.

Morgan starts giggling, softly at first, her shoulders shaking, and it escalates into roaring, table-pounding laughter. She laughs so hard that tears start streaming down her face. We all can't help but join in.

"You're an idiot, Patrick Michael Huff," she finally wheezes. "I'll play along, but I can't wait to see how this blows up in your face eventually."

"Shut up," he tells her with a smile. He and Jade exchange a glance, and I swear I feel a spark pass between them. I'll have to keep an eye on those two.

MORGAN and I are among the last people left as we help clean up and close down the bar for the night.

I watch one of the Velocity staff carry a stack of dishes into the kitchen before I walk over to the bar, where Morgan is wiping everything down for the night.

"Could I trouble you for one last drink before I go?" I ask in my most seductive voice as I slide into my seat.

"Last call was an hour ago," she quips over her shoulder. "But for you, I suppose. What can I get you?"

"I saw there's a drink on special tonight, and it sounded pretty good. Apparently, one of the bartenders here invented it."

She turns around, resting her chin in her hands, with her elbows on the bar top. "Oh yeah?"

"Yeah." I grin at her, this beautiful woman who

makes me proud. The incredible girl I get to call my girlfriend. "I'll take one of those, please."

"One order of Speed Skating coming right up."

I give a little chuckle as she turns around to make her signature cocktail – which she named for me.

If someone would have told me a month ago that I'd be dating Morgan Huff, I wouldn't have believed them. But now, my need for speed only shows up on the ice or on my motorcycle when her arms are wrapped around my waist. Off the ice, I can finally exhale and slow down.

I feel like the luckiest man alive to have two places I can call home. But right now, in this city, in this bar, with the girl I love, there's nowhere else I'd rather be.

THE END

ACKNOWLEDGMENTS

Chris, thanks for taking me for a ride on your motorcycle in 2017. I had so much fun that I came home that night and immediately wrote the scene of Nils taking Morgan on his bike. That was the first thing I ever wrote for this book!

Rachel, we pinky-promised in March 2022 that by the end of the year, we'd have our books published. We didn't succeed. But I'm still proud of us! Thank you for continually motivating me to be a better writer.

Michael, your faith in me and my abilities opened doors and has allowed me to flourish. Thanks for taking a chance on me, and giving me the time, space, and encouragement to work on this manuscript.

Melissa, thank you for believing in indie authors enough to cultivate an entire community of us on Instagram. Your alpha edits and your belief in me gave this book the boost it so desperately needed. Speed

Skating would not have seen the light of day without you. Thank you for everything!

Cait Marie and Jamie, thank you all for the support on the editing and admin side to help me get this book in tip-top shape and out to the readers!

Tacy, I appreciate the Swedish language and culture help! Your insight helped round out Nils. Thank you!

The band Mae, who released Multisensory Aesthetic Experience and spawned a marathon writing session early on in this novel's life. Your music has always reached my heart in a way nothing else has. No matter what I'm feeling, I can always count on your songs to bring inspiration.

Of course, to my dearest husband, thank you for not murdering me when I had Illustrator and Photoshop questions. Graphic design is not my passion. I'm glad to have you there to help me. We make a damn good team.

To everyone else who believed in me, encouraged me, and didn't give me too much shit about how long it took me to publish this book... I appreciate you.

ABOUT THE AUTHOR

Abby Burch had never even seen an NHL game until the Red Wings were in the Stanley Cup Playoffs in 2013. Even though they were eliminated in the Semifinals, Abby was hooked. She attended her first game for her birthday in the 2013-2014 season, and tries to make it to at least one game every year.

When she isn't cheering for the Red Wings or Golden Knights, Abby enjoys running her wedding photography business, traveling, watching videos of other people playing video games, doing random arts and crafts, and being an advocate for type 1 diabetes awareness, a condition which she was diagnosed with in 2012.

You can find more of Abby on Instagram @abbyburch.author, and on her wedding photography website, lewayneproductions.com.

Printed in Great Britain
by Amazon